SENSE & SENSIBILITY
The SCREENPLAY

JANE AUSTEN'S
Sense &
Sensibility

The Screenplay by
EMMA THOMPSON

BLOOMSBURY

ACKNOWLEDGEMENTS

I should like to acknowledge the profoundest debt (for my having developed any sense of humour) to Jane Austen, Monty Python and The Magic Roundabout.

This paperback edition published 1996

Bloomsbury Publishing Plc, 2 Soho Square, London W1V 6HB

A CIP catalogue record for this book is availiable from the British Library.

2 4 6 8 10 9 7 5 3 1

ISBN 0 7475 2860 8

Typeset by Hewer Text Composition Services, Edinburgh
Printed in Great Britain by Cox & Wyman, Reading

SENSE & SENSIBILITY
The SCREENPLAY

0 EXT. OPEN ROADS. NIGHT. TITLE SEQUENCE.
A series of travelling shots. A well-dressed, pompous-looking individual (JOHN DASHWOOD, 35) is making an urgent journey on horseback. He looks anxious.

1 EXT. NORLAND PARK. ENGLAND. MARCH 1800. NIGHT.
Silence. Norland Park, a large country house built in the early part of the eighteenth century, lies in the moonlit parkland.

2 INT. NORLAND PARK. MR DASHWOOD'S BEDROOM. NIGHT.
In the dim light shed by candles we see a bed in which a MAN (MR DASHWOOD, 52) lies – his skin waxy, his breathing laboured. Around him two silhouettes move and murmur, their clothing susurrating in the deathly hush. DOCTORS. A WOMAN (MRS DASHWOOD, 50) sits by his side, holding his hand, her eyes never leaving his face.

> MR DASHWOOD (*urgent*)
> Is John not yet arrived?

> MRS DASHWOOD
> We expect him at any moment, dearest.

MR DASHWOOD looks anguished.

> MR DASHWOOD
> The girls – I have left so little.

> MRS DASHWOOD
> Shh, hush, Henry.

> MR DASHWOOD
> Elinor will try to look after you all, but make sure she finds a good husband. The men are such noodles hereabouts, little wonder none has pleased her.

They smile at each other. MRS DASHWOOD is just managing to conceal her fear and grief.

MRS DASHWOOD
But Marianne is sure to find her storybook hero.

MR DASHWOOD
A romantic poet with flashing eyes and empty pockets?

MRS DASHWOOD
As long as she loves him, who*ever* he is.

MR DASHWOOD
Margaret will go to sea and become a pirate so we need not concern ourselves with her.

MRS DASHWOOD *tries to laugh but it emerges as a sob. An older* MANSERVANT (THOMAS) *now enters, anxiety written on every feature.*

THOMAS
Your son is arrived from London, sir.

MR DASHWOOD *squeezes his wife's hand.*

MR DASHWOOD
Let me speak to John alone.

She nods quickly and he smiles at her with infinite tenderness.

MR DASHWOOD
Ah, my dear. How happy you have made me.

MRS DASHWOOD *makes a superhuman effort and smiles back. She allows* THOMAS *to help her out. She passes* JOHN DASHWOOD *as he enters, presses his hand, but cannot speak.* JOHN *takes her place by the bed.*

JOHN
Father . . .

MR DASHWOOD *summons his last ounces of energy and starts to whisper with desperate intensity.*

———

2

MR DASHWOOD

John – you will find out soon enough from my will that the estate of Norland was left to me in such a way as prevents me from dividing it between my families.

JOHN *blinks. He cannot quite take it in.*

JOHN

Calm yourself, Father. This is not good for you –

But MR DASHWOOD *continues with even greater determination.*

MR DASHWOOD

Norland in its entirety is therefore yours by law and I am happy for you and Fanny.

JOHN *looks torn between genuine distress and unexpected delight.*

MR DASHWOOD

But your stepmother – my wife – and daughters are left with only five hundred pounds a year, barely enough to live on and nothing for the girls' dowries. You must help them.

JOHN's *face is a picture of conflicting emotions. Behind them is the ominous rustling of parchments.*

JOHN

Of course –

MR DASHWOOD

You must promise to do this.

A brief moment of sincerity overcomes JOHN's *natural hypocrisy.*

JOHN

I promise, Father, I promise.

MR DASHWOOD *seems relieved. Suddenly his breathing changes.* JOHN *looks alarmed. He rises and we hear him going to find the* DOCTOR.

―――――

JOHN

Come! Come quickly!

But it is we who share the dying man's last words.

MR DASHWOOD

Help them . . .

3 EXT. JOHN AND FANNY'S TOWN HOUSE. LONDON. DAY.
Outside the house sits a very well-to-do carriage. Behind it waits another open carriage upon which servants are laying trunks and boxes.

FANNY (V/O)

'Help them?'

4 INT. JOHN AND FANNY'S TOWN HOUSE. DRESSING ROOM. DAY.
JOHN is standing in mourning clothes and a travelling cape. He is watching, and obviously waiting for, a pert WOMAN (FANNY DASHWOOD) who is standing by a mirror looking at him keenly.

FANNY

What do you mean, 'help them'?

JOHN

Dearest, I mean to give them three thousand pounds.

FANNY goes very still. JOHN gets nervous.

JOHN

The interest will provide them with a little extra income. Such a gift will certainly discharge my promise to my father.

FANNY slowly turns back to the mirror.

FANNY

Oh, without question! More than amply . . .

JOHN

One had rather, on such occasions, do too much than too little.

———

A pause as FANNY *turns and looks at him again.*

                    JOHN
          Of course, he did not stipulate a particular sum . . .

5 INT. LAUNDRY. NORLAND PARK. DAY.
A red-eyed MAID (BETSY) *plunges a beautiful muslin frock into a vat of black dye.*

6 INT. NORLAND PARK. MRS DASHWOOD'S BEDROOM. DAY.
MRS DASHWOOD *is rushing about, mourning ribbons flapping, putting her knick-knacks into a small valise. The room is in chaos. A young* WOMAN (ELINOR DASHWOOD) *looks on helplessly.*

                    MRS DASHWOOD
          To be reduced to the condition of visitor in my own home! It is
          not to be borne, Elinor!

                    ELINOR
          Consider, Mamma! We have nowhere to go.

                    MRS DASHWOOD
          John and Fanny will descend from London at any moment,
          followed no doubt by cartloads of relatives ready to turn us out
          of our rooms one by one – do you expect me to be here to
          welcome them? Vultures!

She suddenly collapses into a chair and bursts into tears.

                    ELINOR
          I shall start making enquiries for a new house at once. Until
          then we must try to bear their coming.

7 INT. JOHN AND FANNY'S CARRIAGE. DAY.
JOHN *and* FANNY *are on their way out of London.*

                    JOHN
          Fifteen hundred then. What say you to fifteen hundred?

———

FANNY

What brother on earth would do half so much for his real sisters
– let alone half-blood?

JOHN

They can hardly expect more.

FANNY

There is no knowing what they expect. The question is, what
can you afford?

8 INT. NORLAND PARK. DRAWING ROOM. DAY.
*A beautiful young WOMAN (MARIANNE DASHWOOD) is sitting at the
piano playing a particularly sad piece. ELINOR enters.*

ELINOR

Marianne, cannot you play something else? Mamma has been
weeping since breakfast.

MARIANNE *stops, turns the pages of her music book and starts playing
something equally lugubrious.*

ELINOR

I meant something less mournful, dearest.

9 EXT. ROADSIDE INN. DAY.
JOHN *and* FANNY *are waiting as the* OSTLERS *make the final adjustments
to their carriage. The* LANDLORD *hovers, waiting for a tip.*

JOHN

A hundred pounds a year to their mother while she lives. Would
that be more advisable? It is better than parting with the fifteen
hundred all at once.

He displays some coins in his hand. FANNY *removes one and nods.*

FANNY

But if she should live longer than fifteen years we would be

———

completely taken in. People always live forever when there is an annuity to be paid them.

JOHN *gives the coins to the* LANDLORD.

10 EXT. NORLAND PARK. MARGARET'S TREE-HOUSE. DAY.
ELINOR *comes to the foot of a large tree from which a small staircase issues.*

> ELINOR
> Margaret, are you there? Please come down. John and Fanny will be here soon.

A pause. ELINOR *is about to leave when a disembodied and truculent young voice stops her.*

> MARGARET (V/O)
> Why are they coming to live at Norland? They already have a house in London.

> ELINOR
> Because houses go from father to son, dearest – not from father to daughter. It is the law.

Silence. ELINOR *tries another tack.*

> ELINOR
> If you come inside, we could play with your atlas.

> MARGARET (V/O)
> It's not my atlas any more. It's their atlas.

CLOSE *on* ELINOR *as she ponders the truth of this statement.*

11 INT. JOHN AND FANNY'S CARRIAGE. DAY.
JOHN *and* FANNY *joggle on.*

> JOHN
> Twenty pounds now and then will amply discharge my promise, you are quite right.

7

FANNY

Indeed. Although to say the truth, I am convinced within myself that your father had no idea of your giving them money.

JOHN

They will have five hundred a year amongst them as it is –

FANNY

– and what on earth can four women want for more than that? Their housekeeping will be nothing at all – they will have no carriage, no horses, hardly any servants and will keep no company. Only conceive how comfortable they will be!

12 INT. NORLAND PARK. SERVANTS' HALL. DAY.
The large contingent of SERVANTS *who staff Norland Park are gathered in gloomy silence as* ELINOR *addresses them.*

ELINOR

As you know, we are looking for a new home. When we leave we shall be able to retain only Thomas and Betsy.

CAM *holds on* THOMAS *and* BETSY, *a capable woman.*

ELINOR (*cont.*)

We are very sorry to have to leave you all. But we are certain you will find the new Mrs Dashwood a fair and generous mistress.

13 EXT. NORLAND PARK. DRIVE. DAY.
JOHN *and* FANNY's *carriage approaches Norland.*

FANNY (V/O)

They will be much more able to give *you* something.

14 INT. JOHN AND FANNY'S CARRIAGE. DAY.
JOHN *and* FANNY *are about to get out.*

JOHN

So – we are agreed. No money – but the occasional gift of game and fish in season will be very welcome.

FANNY

Your father would be proud of you.

15 INT. NORLAND PARK. DINING ROOM. EARLY EVE.
The entire family, with the exception of MARGARET, is present. BETSY is serving food in an atmosphere of stiff silence. Cutlery clinks. JOHN chews loudly. MARIANNE is rigid with resentment. MRS DASHWOOD maintains a cool, removed dignity. ELINOR tries to play hostess.

ELINOR

How is Mrs Ferrars?

FANNY

My mother is always in excellent health, thank you. My brother Robert is in town with her this season and quite the most popular bachelor in London! He has his own barouche.

In the brief silence which follows this, FANNY surreptitiously checks the hallmark on her butterknife.

ELINOR

You have two brothers, have you not?

FANNY

Indeed, yes. Edward is the eldest – Mamma quite depends upon him. He is travelling up from Plymouth shortly and will break his journey here.

MRS DASHWOOD looks at ELINOR pointedly. JOHN notices.

JOHN (*to MRS DASHWOOD*)

If that is agreeable to you, of course.

———

MRS DASHWOOD

My dear John – this is *your* home now.

FANNY *looks about, barely able to conceal her satisfaction.*

16 INT. NORLAND PARK. ELINOR'S BEDROOM. DAY.
ELINOR *is sitting with a little pile of parcels. She puts a shawl into some paper and ties it with ribbon as* MARIANNE *thunders in, looking mutinous.*

MARIANNE

Fanny wishes to know where the key for the silver cabinet is kept.

ELINOR

Betsy has it, I think. What does Fanny want with the silver?

MARIANNE

I can only presume she wants to count it. What are you doing?

ELINOR

Presents for the servants. Have you seen Margaret? I am worried about her. She has taken to hiding in the oddest places.

MARIANNE

Fortunate girl. At least she can escape Fanny, which is more than any of us is able.

ELINOR

You do your best. You have not said a word to her for a week.

MARIANNE (*truculently*)

I have! I have said 'yes' and 'no'.

17 INT. NORLAND PARK. BREAKFAST ROOM. DAY.
FANNY, MRS DASHWOOD, ELINOR *and* JOHN *are at breakfast.*
MARIANNE *enters.* ELINOR *catches her eye and indicates* FANNY *with a slight motion of her head.* MARIANNE *makes a face.*

MARIANNE (*very polite*)

Good morning, Fanny.

———

FANNY *is rather startled.*

FANNY
Good morning, Marianne.

ELINOR *is relieved.*

MARIANNE *(to Fanny)*
How did you find the silver? Is it all genuine?

ELINOR *rushes in before* MARIANNE *gets any further.*

ELINOR
Pray, when may we expect the pleasure of your brother's company?

FANNY
Edward is due tomorrow. And my dear Mrs Dashwood, in view of the fact that he will not be with us for long, I wondered if Miss Margaret would mind giving up her room to him – the view is quite incomparable from her windows and I should so much like Edward to see Norland at its best.

MARIANNE *slams her cup down and throws a furious look at* ELINOR.

18 INT. NORLAND PARK. MARGARET'S BEDROOM. DAY.
ELINOR *and* MARIANNE *are removing* MARGARET's *toys.*

MARIANNE
Intolerable woman!

ELINOR
There is but one consolation – if Edward is anything like Fanny, we shall be only too happy to leave.

19 EXT. NORLAND PARK. DRIVE. DAY.
A very capable HORSEMAN (EDWARD FERRARS) *canters up the gravel drive.* CLOSE *on his face as he gazes up at the elegant façade.*

---

20 INT. NORLAND PARK. DRAWING ROOM. DAY.

Everyone except MARGARET *is present.* EDWARD *has just shaken hands with* ELINOR. *He behaves with great respect to the* DASHWOODS *and seems embarrassed by* FANNY's *proprietorial air.*

> FANNY
>
> But where is Miss Margaret? I declare, Mrs Dashwood, I am beginning to doubt of her existence! She must run positively wild!

> MRS DASHWOOD
>
> Forgive us, Mr Ferrars. My youngest is not to be found this morning. She is a little shy of strangers at present.

> EDWARD
>
> Naturally. I am also shy of strangers and I have nothing like her excuse.

> MARIANNE (*dangerous*)
>
> How do you like your view, Mr Ferrars?

ELINOR *glances at her warningly but* EDWARD *replies with careful consideration.*

> EDWARD
>
> Very much. Your stables are very handsome and beautifully kept, Mrs Dashwood.

> FANNY
>
> Stables! Edward – your windows overlook the lake.

> EDWARD
>
> An – oversight, Fanny, led me to the wrong room. I have rectified the situation and am happily settled in the guest quarters.

MARIANNE *and* ELINOR *look at each other in surprise.* FANNY *looks furious.* MRS DASHWOOD *smiles warmly at* EDWARD. CLOSE *on* ELINOR. *She is impressed.*

———

21 INT. NORLAND PARK. STAIRCASE. DAY.

FANNY *is walking with* EDWARD, *who looks at the pictures with interest.*

FANNY

They are all exceedingly spoilt, I find. Miss Margaret spends all her time up trees and under furniture and I have barely had a civil word from Marianne.

EDWARD

My dear Fanny, they have just lost their father – their lives will never be the same again.

FANNY

That is no excuse.

22 INT. NORLAND PARK. LIBRARY. DAY.

FANNY *leads* EDWARD *in. She sniffs with distaste.*

FANNY

I have never liked the smell of books.

EDWARD

Oh? No. The dust, perhaps.

As they speak, EDWARD *notices a large atlas retreating apparently all by itself across the floor. Someone is obviously under the table, pulling it out of sight. He registers it and immediately moves in such a way as to shield it from* FANNY. *He turns back, searching for something to divert her.*

EDWARD

I hear you have great plans for the walnut grove.

FANNY

Oh yes! I shall have it pulled down to make room for a Grecian temple.

There is a stifled wail from under the table, which EDWARD *covers with a cough.*

———

EDWARD

How picturesque. Will you show me the site?

And he ushers FANNY *out, flicking a quick glance over his shoulder at the fugitive's foot.*

23 INT. NORLAND PARK. VELVET ROOM. DAY.
ELINOR, MRS DASHWOOD *and* MARIANNE *are sitting round a table with a pile of letters.* ELINOR *is handing one back to her mother.*

ELINOR

Too expensive. We do not need four bedrooms, we can share.

MARIANNE

This one, then?

ELINOR *reads the letter quickly.*

ELINOR

Marianne, we have only five hundred pounds a year. I will send out more enquiries today.

There is a knock on the door. Hesitantly, EDWARD *appears.*

EDWARD

Pardon my intrusion, but I believe I have found what you are looking for . . .

MARIANNE *and* MRS DASHWOOD *are puzzled by his elliptical manner but* ELINOR *immediately understands and rises, in smiling relief.*

24 INT. NORLAND PARK. ENTRANCE HALL OUTSIDE LIBRARY. DAY.
EDWARD *is standing outside keeping a discreet lookout. The door is half open and he can hear* ELINOR *trying to coax* MARGARET *out.* FANNY *walks by with a* BUTLER *to whom she is giving instructions.* EDWARD *pretends to examine the mouldings and she passes on unsuspecting.*

ELINOR (V/O)

Won't you come out, dearest? We haven't seen you all day. Mamma is very concerned.

More silence. EDWARD thinks hard. He makes a decision.

25 INT. NORLAND PARK. LIBRARY. DAY.
EDWARD *walks in loudly.*

EDWARD

Oh, Miss Dashwood! Excuse me – I was wondering – do you by any chance have such a thing as a reliable atlas?

ELINOR *looks up at him in astonishment.*

ELINOR

I believe so.

EDWARD

Excellent. I wish to check the position of the Nile.

EDWARD *appears to be utterly sincere.*

EDWARD

My sister says it is in South America.

From under the table we hear a snort. ELINOR looks at him in realisation.

ELINOR

Oh! No, no indeed. She is quite wrong. For I believe it is in – in – Belgium.

EDWARD

Belgium? Surely not. You must be thinking of the Volga.

MARGARET (*from under the table*)
The Volga?

ELINOR

Of course. The Volga, which, as you know, starts in –

15

EDWARD

Vladivostok, and ends in –

ELINOR

St Albans.

EDWARD

Indeed. Where the coffee beans come from . . .

They are having such a good time that it is rather a pity the game is stopped by the appearance from under the table of MARGARET who reveals herself to be a dishevelled girl of eleven. She hauls the atlas up and plonks it in front of EDWARD.

MARGARET

The source of the Nile is in Abyssinia.

EDWARD

Is it? Good heavens. How do you do. Edward Ferrars.

MARGARET

Margaret Dashwood.

EDWARD *shakes MARGARET's hand solemnly and looks over her head at ELINOR. They smile at each other, a connection made.*

26 INT. NORLAND PARK. DRAWING ROOM. ANOTHER DAY.
JOHN *is reading a newspaper. MRS DASHWOOD sits across from FANNY, who thumbs through a fashion-plate magazine. ELINOR is at a desk by the window writing a letter – we see the words 'of course we should like to leave as soon as possible'. Suddenly she hears a commotion outside. MARGARET runs past the window brandishing a stick. EDWARD follows, and proceeds to teach her the first principles of sword-fighting. They feint and parry, EDWARD serious and without a hint of condescension, MAR-GARET concentrating furiously. EDWARD suddenly turns, as though feeling ELINOR's gaze. She smiles but looks away quickly.*

---

27 INT. NORLAND PARK. VELVET ROOM. ANOTHER DAY.

EDWARD *comes into the doorway and sees* ELINOR *who is listening to* MARIANNE *playing a concerto.* ELINOR *stands in a graceful, rather sad attitude, her back to us. Suddenly she senses* EDWARD *behind her and turns. He is about to turn away, embarrassed to have been caught admiring her, when he sees she has been weeping. Hastily she tries to dry her eyes. He comes forward and offers her a handkerchief, which she takes with a grateful smile. We notice his monogram in the corner: ECF.*

> ELINOR (*apologetic*)
> That was my father's favourite.

EDWARD *nods kindly.*

> ELINOR
> Thank you so much for your help with Margaret, Mr Ferrars. She is a changed girl since your arrival.

> EDWARD
> Not at all. I enjoy her company.

> ELINOR
> Has she shown you her tree-house?

> EDWARD
> Not yet. Would you do me the honour, Miss Dashwood? It is very fine out.

> ELINOR
> With pleasure.

They start to walk out of shot, still talking.

> ELINOR
> Margaret has always wanted to travel.

> EDWARD
> I know. She is heading an expedition to China shortly. I am to

go as her servant but only on the understanding that I will be very badly treated.

ELINOR

What will your duties be?

EDWARD

Sword-fighting, administering rum and swabbing.

ELINOR

Ah.

CAM *tilts up to find* MRS DASHWOOD *on the middle landing of the staircase, smiling down at them.* CAM *tilts up yet further to find* FANNY *on the landing above, watching* EDWARD *and* ELINOR *with a face like a prune.*

28 EXT. NORLAND PARK. GARDENS. DAY.
EDWARD *and* ELINOR *are still talking as they walk arm in arm in the late-afternoon sun.*

EDWARD

All I want – all I have ever wanted – is the quiet of a private life but my mother is determined to see me distinguished.

ELINOR

As?

EDWARD

She hardly knows. Any fine figure will suit – a great orator, a leading politician, even a barrister would serve, but only on the condition that I drive my own barouche and dine in the first circles.

His tone is light but there is an underlying bitterness to it.

ELINOR

And what do you wish for?

EDWARD

I always preferred the church, but that is not smart enough for
my mother – she prefers the army, but that is a great deal too
smart for me.

ELINOR

Would you stay in London?

EDWARD

I hate London. No peace. A country living is my ideal – a small
parish where I might do some good, keep chickens and give very
short sermons.

30 EXT. FIELDS NEAR NORLAND. DAY.

EDWARD *and* ELINOR *are on horseback. The atmosphere is intimate, the
quality of the conversation rooted now in their affections.*

ELINOR

You talk of feeling idle and useless – imagine how that is
compounded when one has no choice and no hope whatsoever
of any occupation.

EDWARD *nods and smiles at the irony of it.*

EDWARD

Our circumstances are therefore precisely the same.

ELINOR

Except that you will inherit your fortune.

He looks at her slightly shocked but enjoying her boldness.

ELINOR (*cont.*)

We cannot even earn ours.

EDWARD

Perhaps Margaret is right.

———

ELINOR

Right?

EDWARD

Piracy is our only option.

They ride on in silence for a moment.

EDWARD (*cont.*)

What *is* swabbing exactly?

31 INT. NORLAND PARK. DRAWING ROOM. EVE.

Dinner is over. JOHN and FANNY are examining plans of the Norland estate, looking for somewhere to build a hermitage. EDWARD is reading out loud. ELINOR embroiders and listens. MRS DASHWOOD and MAR-IANNE make up the rest of the audience, the latter in a state of high impatience.

EDWARD

No voice divine the storm allayed
No light propitious shone,
When snatched from all effectual aid,
We perished each alone:
But I beneath a rougher sea,
And whelmed in deeper gulfs than he.

MARIANNE *jumps up and goes to him.*

MARIANNE

No, Edward! Listen –

She takes the book from him and reads the stanza with passionate brio.

MARIANNE

Can you not feel his despair? Try again.

Rather mortified, EDWARD starts again, but not before receiving a sympathetic look from ELINOR which seems to comfort him a little.

———

32 INT. NORLAND PARK. MORNING ROOM. DAY

MRS DASHWOOD *is ruminating sadly.* MARIANNE *rushes in holding a letter.*

> MARIANNE
>
> Mamma, look. This has just arrived.

> MRS DASHWOOD (*reading from the letter*)
>
> 'I should be pleased to offer you a home at Barton Cottage as soon as ever you have need of it' – why, it is from my cousin, Sir John Middleton!

> MARIANNE
>
> Even Elinor must approve the rent.

MRS DASHWOOD *looks at the letter again and thinks.*

> MRS DASHWOOD
>
> Has Elinor not yet seen this?

> MARIANNE
>
> No – I will fetch her.

> MRS DASHWOOD
>
> Wait. No. Let us delay.

> MARIANNE
>
> Why?

> MRS DASHWOOD
>
> I think – I believe – that Edward and Elinor have formed an attachment.

Marianne nods, a little reluctantly.

> MRS DASHWOOD
>
> It would be cruel to take her away so soon – and Devonshire is so far.

———

MRS DASHWOOD *makes her decision. She takes the letter and hides it in the pocket of her gown.* MARIANNE *looks on frowningly.*

MRS DASHWOOD
Why so grave? Do you disapprove her choice?

MARIANNE
By no means. Edward is very amiable.

MRS DASHWOOD
Amiable – but?

MARIANNE
But there is something wanting. He is too sedate – his reading last night . . .

MRS DASHWOOD
Elinor has not your feelings, his reserve suits her.

MARIANNE *thinks for a little.*

MARIANNE
Can he love her? Can the ardour of the soul really be satisfied with such polite, concealed affections? To love is to burn – to be on fire, all made of passion, of adoration, of sacrifice! Like Juliet, or Guinevere or Heloïse –

MRS DASHWOOD
They made rather pathetic ends, dear.

MARIANNE
Pathetic! To die for love? How can you say so? What could be more glorious?

MRS DASHWOOD
I think that may be taking your romantic sensibilities a little far . . .

———

MARIANNE

The more I know of the world, the more I am convinced that I shall never see a man whom I can truly love.

MRS DASHWOOD

You require so much!

MARIANNE

I do not! I require only what any young woman of taste should – a man who sings well, dances admirably, rides bravely, reads with passion and whose tastes agree in every point with my own.

33 INT. NORLAND PARK. ELINOR'S BEDROOM. NIGHT.
ELINOR *is in bed, deep in thought.* MARIANNE *enters in her nightclothes, carrying a book of poetry. She reads, teasingly.*

MARIANNE

Is love a fancy, or a feeling? No
It is immortal as immaculate truth
'Tis not a blossom shed as soon as Youth
Drops from the stem of life – for it will grow
In barren regions, where no waters flow
Nor ray of promise cheats the pensive gloom –

She jumps onto the bed. ELINOR *smiles – somewhat suspiciously.*

MARIANNE

What a pity it is that Edward has no passion for reading.

ELINOR

It was you who asked him to read – and then you made him nervous.

MARIANNE

Me?

———

ELINOR

But your behaviour to him in all other respects is perfectly cordial so I must assume that you like him in spite of his deficiencies.

MARIANNE (*trying hard*)

I think him everything that is amiable and worthy.

ELINOR

Praise indeed!

MARIANNE

But he shall have my unanswering devotion when you tell me he is to be my brother . . .

ELINOR *is greatly taken aback and does not know how to reply. Suddenly* MARIANNE *hugs her passionately.*

MARIANNE

How shall I do without you?

ELINOR

Do without me?

MARIANNE *pulls away, her eyes full of tears.*

MARIANNE

I am sure you will be very happy. But you must promise not to live *too* far away.

ELINOR

Marianne, there is no question of – that is, there is no understanding between . . .

ELINOR *trails off.* MARIANNE *looks at her keenly.*

MARIANNE

Do you love him?

The bold clarity of this question discomforts ELINOR.

———

ELINOR

I do not attempt to deny that I think very highly of him – that I greatly esteem – that I *like* him.

MARIANNE

Esteem him! Like him! Use those insipid words again and I shall leave the room this instant!

This makes ELINOR *laugh in spite of her discomfort.*

ELINOR

Very well. Forgive me. Believe my feelings to be stronger than I have declared – but further than that you must not believe.

MARIANNE *is flummoxed but she rallies swiftly and picks up her book again.*

MARIANNE

'Is love a fancy or a feeling?' Or a Ferrars?

ELINOR

Go to bed!

ELINOR *blushes in good earnest.* MARIANNE *goes to the door.*

MARIANNE (*imitating Elinor*)
'I do not attempt to deny that I think highly of him – greatly esteem him! *Like* him!'

And she is gone, leaving ELINOR *both agitated and amused.*

34 INT. NORLAND PARK. BREAKFAST ROOM. DAY.
FANNY *is standing by the window looking out. We see her POV of* ELINOR *and* EDWARD *walking in the garden.* MRS DASHWOOD *enters, pauses for a moment and then joins* FANNY *at the window.* FANNY *pretends not to have been watching but* MRS DASHWOOD *looks down at the lovers and then smiles sweetly at her.*

MRS DASHWOOD

We are all so happy that you chose to invite Edward to Norland. He is a dear boy and we are all very fond of him.

FANNY *does a bit of quick thinking.*

FANNY

We have great hopes for him. Much is expected of him by our mother with regard to his profession –

MRS DASHWOOD

Naturally.

FANNY

And in marriage. She is determined that both he and Robert will marry well.

MRS DASHWOOD

Of course. But I hope she desires them to marry for love, first and foremost? I have always felt that, contrary to common wisdom, true affection is by far the most valuable dowry.

FANNY

Love is all very well, but unfortunately we cannot always rely on the heart to lead us in the most suitable directions.

FANNY *lowers her voice confidingly.*

FANNY

You see, my dear Mrs Dashwood, Edward is entirely the kind of compassionate person upon whom penniless women can prey – and having entered into any kind of understanding, he would never go back on his word. He is quite simply incapable of doing so. But it would lead to his ruin. I worry for him so, Mrs Dashwood. My mother has always made it perfectly plain that she will withdraw all financial support from Edward, should he choose to plant his affections in less . . . exalted ground than he deserves.

It is impossible for MRS DASHWOOD *not to get the point. She is appalled and furious.*

———

MRS DASHWOOD

I understand you perfectly.

She sweeps off.

35 INT. NORLAND PARK. MRS DASHWOOD'S DRESSING ROOM.
DAY.

MRS DASHWOOD, *breathless with rage, is searching through her wardrobe for the gown which contains* SIR JOHN's *letter. Frocks fly hither and thither. Finally* MRS DASHWOOD *plunges her hand into the right pocket and withdraws the letter. She looks at it, suddenly concerned and anxious.*

36 INT. NORLAND PARK. DINING ROOM. EVE.

The entire family is present. Everyone is watching MRS DASHWOOD, *who has just made her announcement.*

EDWARD

Devonshire!

He is devastated. FANNY *is thrilled.* MRS DASHWOOD *looks at him with compassion and then at* ELINOR, *who is trying to keep calm.*

MRS DASHWOOD

My cousin Sir John Middleton has offered us a small house on his estate.

JOHN

Sir John Middleton? What is his situation? He must be a man of property.

MRS DASHWOOD

He is a widower. He lives with his mother-in-law at Barton Park and it is Barton Cottage that he offers us.

FANNY

Oh, a cottage! How charming. A little cottage is always very snug.

———

EDWARD

But you will not leave before the summer?

MRS DASHWOOD

Oh, my dear Edward, we can no longer trespass upon your sister's good will. We must leave as soon as possible.

MARGARET

You will come and stay with us, Edward!

EDWARD

I should like that very much.

FANNY

Edward has long been expected in town by our mother.

MRS DASHWOOD *ignores* FANNY.

MRS DASHWOOD

Come as soon as you can, Edward. Remember that you are always welcome.

37 INT/EXT. NORLAND PARK. STABLES. DAY.
ELINOR *has come to say goodbye to her* HORSE. *She strokes the soft face sadly. Then she senses someone and turns to find* EDWARD *standing nearby.*

EDWARD

Cannot you take him with you?

ELINOR

We cannot possibly afford him.

EDWARD

Perhaps he could make himself useful in the kitchen?

ELINOR *tries to smile.* EDWARD *looks at her for a long moment and then comes closer.*

EDWARD

Miss Dashwood – Elinor. I must talk to you.

The use of her Christian name – and in such a loving tone – stops ELINOR's breath altogether.

EDWARD

There is something of great importance I need . . . to tell you –

He comes closer still. The HORSE breathes between them. ELINOR is on fire with anticipation but EDWARD looks troubled and has less the air of a suitor than he might.

EDWARD

– about – about my education.

ELINOR (*after a beat*)

Your education?

EDWARD

Yes. It was less . . . successful than it might have been.

EDWARD laughs nervously. ELINOR is completely bewildered.

EDWARD

It was conducted in Plymouth – oddly enough.

ELINOR

Indeed?

EDWARD

Yes. Do you know it?

ELINOR

Plymouth?

EDWARD

Yes.

———

ELINOR

No.

EDWARD

Oh – well – I spent four years there – at a school run by a – a Mr
Pratt –

ELINOR

Pratt?

ELINOR *is beginning to feel like a parrot.*

EDWARD

Precisely – Mr Pratt – and there, I – that is to say, he has a –

As EDWARD *flounders, a familiar voice cuts through this unexpected foray
into his academic past.*

FANNY

Edward! Edward!

They turn to find FANNY *powering down upon them, waving a letter.*
EDWARD *steps back, glancing almost guiltily at* ELINOR, *who is as
confused as we are.*

FANNY

I have been all over for you! You are needed in London this instant!

EDWARD

Fanny, I am leaving this afternoon as it is –

FANNY

No, no, that will not do. Family affairs are in chaos owing to
your absence. Mother is quite adamant that you should leave at
once.

FANNY *is determined. She obviously has no intention of leaving him alone
with* ELINOR. EDWARD *turns to* ELINOR, *frustration in every muscle, his
jaw set tight.*

EDWARD

Excuse me, Miss Dashwood.

FANNY *drags* EDWARD *off, leaving* ELINOR *to gaze sadly after them.*

39 INT. THE LADIES' CARRIAGE. OPEN ROAD. RAIN. EVE.
The DASHWOODS *are on their way. The mood is very sombre.*

MARGARET

Edward promised he would bring the atlas to Barton for me.

MARIANNE *looks at* ELINOR, *pleased.*

MARIANNE

Did he? Well, I will wager he will do so in less than a fortnight!

MRS DASHWOOD *looks at* ELINOR *with satisfaction.*

40 EXT. THE LADIES' CARRIAGE. OPEN ROAD. EVE.
The carriage rolls on.

MARGARET (V/O)

Are we there yet?

41 EXT. ROAD TO AND FROM BARTON COTTAGE. DAY.
In comparison to Norland, Barton Cottage has the air of a damp shoebox. It sits low and bleak in the grey lonely countryside.

From one side we can see the DASHWOODS' *carriage drawing up at the gate. From the other, a much grander vehicle, from which loud whooping can be heard, is approaching.*

42 EXT. BARTON COTTAGE. GARDEN PATH. DAY.
As the exhausted DASHWOODS *alight, they converge with a ruddy-complexioned* MAN *in a redingote* (SIR JOHN MIDDLETON) *and a rotund, equally roseate* LADY (MRS JENNINGS) *who have fallen over each other in their haste to get out of their carriage.*

MRS DASHWOOD
Sir John!

SIR JOHN *clasps her hands and starts to help her up the path, followed by* ELINOR, MARIANNE *and* MARGARET, *who is clearly fascinated by his bouncy companion.*

SIR JOHN
Dear ladies, dear ladies, upon my word, here you are, here you are, here you are!

MRS DASHWOOD
Sir John, your extraordinary kindness –

SIR JOHN
Oh, none of that, hush, please, none of that, but here is my dear mamma-in-law Mrs Jennings.

MRS JENNINGS
Was the journey tolerable, you poor souls?

SIR JOHN
Why did you not come up to the Park first and take your ease? We saw you pass –

Like many people who live rather lonely lives together, SIR JOHN *and* MRS JENNINGS *talk incessantly, interrupt each other all the time and never listen.*

MRS JENNINGS
– but I would not wait for you to come to us, I made John call for the carriage –

SIR JOHN
She would not wait, you know.

MRS JENNINGS
– as we get so little company.

––––––

They reach the front door and BETSY's *smiling welcome. In the confusion of milling people and* THOMAS *carrying the lighter luggage,* MARIANNE *contrives to slip into the house alone. We follow her but hear the conversation continuing in* V/O. MARIANNE *looks about the parlour, where a dismal fire is smoking. She starts up the stairs, expressionless.*

> MRS JENNINGS (V/O)
>
> But I feel as if I know you already – delightful creatures!

> SIR JOHN (V/O)
>
> Delightful! And you know you are to dine at Barton Park every day.

> MRS DASHWOOD (V/O)
>
> Oh, but dear Sir John, we cannot –

> SIR JOHN (V/O)
>
> Oh, no no no no no no no, I shall not brook refusals. I am quite deaf to 'em, you know –

> MRS JENNINGS (V/O)
>
> – deaf –

MARIANNE *enters a small bedroom. She sits on the bed. Then she goes to the window and opens it. Voices float up.*

> SIR JOHN (V/O)
>
> But I insist!

> ELINOR (V/O)
>
> Let us only settle in for a few days, Sir John, and thank you –

> SIR JOHN (V/O)
>
> Oh, no thankings, no, please, can't bear 'em, embarrassing, you know –

MARIANNE *closes the window and crosses the corridor to another bedroom – similarly stark. She sighs and turns back down the stairs.*

———

SIR JOHN (V/O)

We will send game and fruit as a matter of course –

MRS JENNINGS (V/O)

– fruit and game –

SIR JOHN (V/O)

– and the carriage is at your beck and call –

MARIANNE *joins the group, who are now in the parlour.*

MRS JENNINGS

– call – and here is Miss Marianne!

SIR JOHN

Where did you disappear to?

MRS JENNINGS

I declare you are the loveliest girl I ever set eyes on! Cannot you get them married, Mrs Dashwood? You must not leave it too long!

SIR JOHN

But, alas, there are no smart young men hereabouts to woo them –

MRS JENNINGS

– not a beau for miles!

The strain of exhibiting joy and gratitude is beginning to tell on MRS DASHWOOD *who is sagging visibly.*

SIR JOHN

Come, Mother, let us leave them in peace.

MRS JENNINGS

But there is Colonel Brandon!

SIR JOHN *is dragging her down the path.*

———

SIR JOHN

Excellent fellow! We served in the East India Regiment
together.

MRS JENNINGS

Just wait till he sees you! If we can persuade him out to meet
you!

SIR JOHN

Reclusive individual. But you are fatigued. I can see that you are
fatigued.

Now he is pushing her into the carriage.

MRS JENNINGS

Of course she is fatigued!

SIR JOHN

Come along, Mother, we really must leave them to themselves.

MRS JENNINGS

You must get your maidservant to make you up some camphor
– it is the best tonic for the staggers!

SIR JOHN

Send Thomas to us for the carriage when you are ready!

They take off, waving wildly. MARGARET *goes down the path to watch
them and turns back to her slightly stunned family.*

MARGARET

I like *them.*

MRS DASHWOOD (*weakly*)

What generosity.

ELINOR

Indeed. I am surprised they did not offer us their clothing.

———

43 INT. BARTON COTTAGE. ELINOR AND MARIANNE'S
BEDROOM. NIGHT.
MARIANNE *and* ELINOR *are getting undressed for bed. It's very cold.
They keep their underclothing on and get in, shivering at the bony chill of the
linen.*

44 EXT. BARTON COTTAGE. KITCHEN GARDEN. DAY.
BETSY *is pinning out laundry.*

45 EXT. BARTON COTTAGE. GARDEN. DAY.
MARGARET *tries to climb an impossible tree. Her petticoats snag and tear.*

46 INT. BARTON COTTAGE. ELINOR AND MARIANNE'S
BEDROOM. DAY.
MARIANNE *looks out of the window at the wild countryside. Unconsciously,
one hand plays up and down on the sill as though it were a keyboard.*

47 INT. BARTON COTTAGE. PARLOUR. DAY.
ELINOR *sits at a little desk counting money and making notes.* BETSY
enters to clean out the fire. She notices the money.

BETSY

> Sugar is five shilling a pound these parts, Miss Dashwood.

ELINOR (lightly)

> No more sugar then.

48 INT. BARTON COTTAGE. PARLOUR. EVE.
CLOSE *on* MRS DASHWOOD *looking out of the window, thinking. She
remembers* MRS JENNINGS's *words*:

MRS JENNINGS (V/O)

> Not a beau for miles . . .

MRS DASHWOOD *turns into the room to look at her brood.* ELINOR *and*
MARIANNE *are mending* MARGARET's *petticoats.* CLOSE *on the
mother's anxious expression – what is to become of them?*

---

49 EXT. BARTON PARK. EVE.

Establishing shot of SIR JOHN's house – a very comfortable-looking country seat with fine grounds.

> ### SIR JOHN (V/O)
> Where can Brandon be, poor fellow? I hope he has not lamed his horse.

50 INT. BARTON PARK. DINING ROOM. EVE.

CLOSE *on an empty chair and place setting. Pull out to reveal the DASH-WOODS at their first dinner with SIR JOHN and MRS JENNINGS.*

> ### MRS JENNINGS
> Colonel Brandon is the most eligible bachelor in the county – he is bound to do for one of you. Mind, he is a better age for Miss Dashwood – but I dare say she left her heart behind in Sussex, eh?

MARIANNE *flashes an unmistakable glance of alarmed concern at her sister, which* MRS JENNINGS *notices.*

> ### MRS JENNINGS
> Aha! I see you, Miss Marianne! I think I have unearthed a secret!

> ### SIR JOHN
> Oho! Have you sniffed one out already, Mother? You are worse than my best pointer, Flossie!

They both laugh immoderately. ELINOR *tries to stay calm.*

> ### MRS JENNINGS
> What sort of man is he, Miss Dashwood? Is he butcher, baker, candlestick-maker? I shall winkle it out of you somehow, you know!

> ### SIR JOHN
> She's horribly good at winkling.

MRS JENNINGS
You are in lonely country now, Miss Dashwood, none of us has any secrets here –

SIR JOHN
– or if we do, we do not keep them for long!

ELINOR *tries to smile.* MARIANNE *looks furious.* MARGARET *is staring at* MRS JENNINGS *as if she were some particularly thrilling form of wildlife.*

MRS JENNINGS
He is curate of the parish, I dare say!

SIR JOHN
Or a handsome lieutenant!

MRS JENNINGS
Give us a clue, Miss Dashwood – is he in uniform?

ELINOR *starts to change the subject, but* MARGARET *interrupts her.*

MARGARET
He has no profession!

SIR JOHN *and* MRS JENNINGS *turn on her with screams of delight.* ELINOR, MARIANNE *and* MRS DASHWOOD *look at each other helplessly.*

SIR JOHN
No profession! A gentleman, then!

MARIANNE (*with daggers*)
Margaret, you know perfectly well there is no such person.

MARGARET
There is! There is! And his name begins with an F!

ELINOR *looks hard at her plate.*

MRS DASHWOOD
Margaret!

———

MRS DASHWOOD *is appalled at her youngest's relish for such a vulgar game.* SIR JOHN *and* MRS JENNINGS *are cock-a-hoop.*

> SIR JOHN
> F indeed! A very promising letter. Let me – F, F, Fo, Fa . . . Upon my word, but I cannot think of a single name beginning with F –

> MRS JENNINGS
> Forrest? Foster? Frost? Foggarty?

MARIANNE *suddenly stands up.* SIR JOHN *and* MRS JENNINGS *are so surprised they stop talking. Everyone stares at* MARIANNE.

> MARIANNE (*controlled fury*)
> Sir John, might I play your pianoforte?

> SIR JOHN
> Of course, yes – my goodness. We do not stand on ceremony here, my dear.

For once, ELINOR *is grateful for her sister's rudeness as everyone rises and follows* MARIANNE *out.*

51 EXT. BARTON PARK. FRONT STEPS. EVE.
A soldierly MAN *of about forty* (COLONEL BRANDON) *is dismounting from his horse. From within we hear* MARIANNE's *song begin. His head snaps up to the windows. An expression of pained surprise comes into his melancholy, brooding eyes.*

52 INT. BARTON PARK. MUSIC ROOM. EVE.
Everyone watches MARIANNE *as she plays and sings. Behind them we see* BRANDON *entering. But he stays in the shadow of the door and no one notices him. CLOSE on his face. He gazes at* MARIANNE *with an unfathomable look of grief and longing. He breathes in deeply. Suddenly,* ELINOR *feels his presence and looks around at him. After a few moments, she turns back, slightly puzzled. The song finishes. Everyone claps. The* MAN *ventures out into the light and* SIR JOHN *springs from his seat.*

SIR JOHN

Brandon! Where have you been? Come, come and meet our beautiful new neighbours!

MRS JENNINGS

What a pity you are late, Colonel! You have missed the most delightful singing!

BRANDON *bows to the company and smiles slightly.*

COLONEL BRANDON

A great pity, indeed.

ELINOR *looks at him, even more puzzled.*

SIR JOHN

Mrs Dashwood, may I present my dear friend Colonel Brandon? We served together in the East Indies and I assure you there is no better fellow on earth –

MARGARET

Have you really been to the East Indies, Colonel?

COLONEL BRANDON

I have.

MARGARET

What is it like?

MARGARET *is quivering with fascination.*

SIR JOHN

Like? Hot.

But COLONEL BRANDON *knows what* MARGARET *wants to hear.*

COLONEL BRANDON (*mysteriously*)

The air is full of spices.

MARGARET *smiles with satisfaction.*

————

SIR JOHN

Come, Miss Dashwood – it is your turn to entertain us!

ELINOR

Oh no, Sir John, I do not –

SIR JOHN

– and I think we can all guess what key you will sing in!

SIR JOHN and MRS JENNINGS *are bursting with their new joke.*

SIR JOHN/MRS JENNINGS

F major!

They fall about.

53 INT. SIR JOHN'S CARRIAGE. NIGHT.
The DASHWOODS are returning home. A row is in progress.

MARIANNE (*to Margaret*)

As for you, you have no right, no right at all, to parade your
ignorant assumptions –

MARGARET

They are not assumptions. You *told* me.

ELINOR *stares at MARIANNE. MARIANNE colours and attacks MAR-
GARET again.*

MARIANNE

I told you nothing –

MARGARET

They'll *meet* him when he comes, anyway.

MARIANNE

That is not the point. You do not speak of such things before
strangers –

———

MARGARET

But everyone *else* was –

MARIANNE

Mrs Jennings is not everyone.

MARGARET

I like her! She talks about things. We never talk about things.

MRS DASHWOOD

Hush, please, now that is enough, Margaret. If you cannot think of anything appropriate to say, you will please restrict your remarks to the weather.

A heated pause.

MARGARET

I like Colonel Brandon too. He's been to places.

54 EXT. POND NEAR BARTON PARK. DAY.
In the background, SIR JOHN, ELINOR *and* MRS JENNINGS *pack the remains of a picnic into a basket.* MRS DASHWOOD *and* MARGARET *examine a foxhole. In the foreground,* MARIANNE *is cutting bulrushes for basketwork. Her knife is blunt and she saws impatiently.* COLONEL BRANDON *materialises at her side and wordlessly offers her his hunting knife. Oddly nervous,* MARIANNE *takes it. She turns back to the rushes and cuts them with ease. The* COLONEL'*s gaze follows her movements as if held by a magnet.*

54A INT. KEEPER'S LODGE. BARTON PARK. DAY.
SIR JOHN *and* BRANDON *are cleaning their guns in companionable silence – a habit left over from army days.* SIR JOHN *eyes* BRANDON *roguishly.*

SIR JOHN

You know what they're saying, of course . . .

No answer.

———

42

SIR JOHN

The word is that you have developed a taste for – certain
company . . .

BRANDON *stays resolutely silent.* SIR JOHN *is emboldened.*

SIR JOHN

And why not, say I. A man like you – in his prime – she'd be a
most fortunate young lady –

BRANDON *cuts across him.*

COLONEL BRANDON

Marianne Dashwood would no more think of me than she
would of *you*, John.

SIR JOHN

Brandon, my boy, do not think of yourself so meanly –

COLONEL BRANDON

And all the better for her.

SIR JOHN *subsides.* BRANDON *is clearly as angry with himself as he is
with* SIR JOHN.

54B EXT. POND NEAR BARTON PARK. ANOTHER DAY.
BRANDON *strides along in hunting gear, a gun slung under one arm, his
dog trotting behind him with a duck clamped between its jaws. The
bulrushes catch his eye and he slows, then stops. He stands for a moment
deep in thought. Then he takes his hunting knife, cuts one and walks off
contemplatively.*

57 EXT. BARTON PARK. GARDENS. DAY.
An outdoor luncheon is in progress. COLONEL BRANDON *is talking to*
MRS DASHWOOD. *Occasionally he looks over towards* MARIANNE, *who
is playing bilboquet with* SIR JOHN *and* MARGARET. MRS JENNINGS
nudges ELINOR *hard and gestures to* BRANDON.

———

MRS JENNINGS (*stage whisper*)

Besotted! Excellent match, for *he* is rich and *she* is handsome.

ELINOR

How long have you known the Colonel?

MRS JENNINGS

Oh, Lord bless you, as long as ever I have been here, and I came fifteen years back. His estate at Delaford is but four miles hence and he and John are very thick. He has no wife or children of his own, for –

MRS JENNINGS *lowers her voice to a stentorian whisper.*

MRS JENNINGS

– he has a tragic history. He loved a girl once – twenty years ago now – a ward to his family, but they were not permitted to marry . . .

ELINOR *is intrigued.*

ELINOR

On what grounds?

MRS JENNINGS

Money. Eliza was poor. When the father discovered their amour, she was flung out of the house and he packed off into the army. I believe he would have done himself a harm if not for John . . .

ELINOR

What became of the lady?

MRS JENNINGS

Oh, she was passed from man to man – disappeared from all good society. When Brandon got back from India he searched for heaven knows how long, only to find her dying in a poor-

---

house. You have seen how it has affected him. Once I thought my daughter Charlotte might have cheered him up, but she is much better off where she is.

ELINOR *is silent with amazement at this unexpected history.*

> MRS JENNINGS
> Look at him *now*, though. So attentive. I shall try an experiment on him.

> ELINOR
> Oh no, please, dear Mrs Jennings, leave the poor Colonel alone.

> MRS JENNINGS
> No, no, it is just the thing – all suitors need a little help, my dear . . .

MRS JENNINGS *winks at* ELINOR *and rubs her hands as though about to perform a magic trick.*

> MRS JENNINGS (*trillingly*)
> Colonel Brandon!

BRANDON *looks up.*

> MRS JENNINGS
> We have not heard you play for us of late!

> COLONEL BRANDON
> For the simple reason that you have a far superior musician here.

He indicates MARIANNE, *who smiles absently.*

> MRS JENNINGS
> Perhaps you did not know, Miss Marianne, that our dear Brandon shares your passion for music and plays the pianoforte very well.

MARIANNE *looks at* BRANDON *in some surprise.*

―――――

MRS JENNINGS

Play us a duet!

BRANDON *looks at* MRS JENNINGS *warningly but she ignores him.*

MRS JENNINGS

I'll trow you know quite as many melancholy tunes as Miss
Marianne!

Her tone is so knowing that MARIANNE *frowns uncomfortably.*

MRS JENNINGS

Come! Let us see you both side by side!

MARIANNE *rises impatiently.*

MARIANNE

I do not know any duets. Forgive me, Colonel.

She moves away. MRS JENNINGS *chuckles.*

58 INT. BARTON COTTAGE. PARLOUR. LATE AFTERNOON.
The DASHWOODS *returning.* MARIANNE *is taking her bonnet off so
furiously that she simply gets the knot tighter and tighter. Despite themselves,* ELINOR *and* MRS DASHWOOD *are amused.*

MARIANNE

Oh! Are we never to have a moment's peace? The rent here may
be low but I think we have it on very hard terms . . .

ELINOR

Mrs Jennings is a wealthy woman with a married daughter –
she has nothing to do but marry off everyone else's.

BETSY *pokes her head out from the dining room.*

BETSY

There's a parcel arrived for you, Miss Dashwood!

MARGARET

A parcel!

They all crowd into the dining room to find a large package on the table, which MARGARET is permitted to open. In the meantime ELINOR comes to the rescue with the bonnet and MARIANNE stands shifting like a spirited mare as ELINOR patiently unravels the knot.

MARIANNE

It is too ridiculous! When is a man to be safe from such wit if age and infirmity do not protect him?

ELINOR

Infirmity!

MRS DASHWOOD

If Colonel Brandon is infirm, then I am at death's door.

ELINOR

It is a miracle your life has extended this far . . .

MARIANNE

Did you not hear him complain of a rheumatism in his shoulder?

ELINOR

'A slight ache' I believe was his phrase . . .

MARIANNE smiles and ELINOR laughs at her. Then MARGARET opens the parcel to reveal – her atlas. The atmosphere alters immediately as MRS DASHWOOD and MARIANNE look at ELINOR in consternation.

MARGARET

But Edward said he would bring it himself.

There is a letter on top of the atlas. CLOSE on the address 'To the Dashwoods'. MRS DASHWOOD picks it up, looks at ELINOR, and opens it.

———

MRS DASHWOOD

'Dear Mrs Dashwood, Miss Dashwood, Miss Marianne and Captain Margaret – it gives me great pleasure to restore this atlas to its rightful owner. Alas, business in London does not permit me to accompany it, although this is likely to hurt me far more than it hurts you. For the present my memories of your kindness must be enough to sustain me, and I remain your devoted servant always. E. C. Ferrars.'

A silence greets this brief epistle. ELINOR *struggles to contain her bitter disappointment.*

MARGARET

But why hasn't he come?

MRS DASHWOOD

He says he is busy, dear.

MARGARET

He *said* he'd come.

MARGARET *is genuinely upset.* ELINOR *quietly hangs up* MARIANNE's *bonnet.*

MARGARET

Why hasn't he come?

MRS DASHWOOD *looks beseechingly at* MARIANNE, *who nods and grasps* MARGARET's *hand.*

MARIANNE

I am taking you for a walk.

MARGARET

No! I've been a walk.

MARIANNE

You need another.

MARGARET

    It is going to rain.

MARIANNE shoves her bonnet back on and drags MARGARET out.

MARIANNE

    It is not going to rain.

MARGARET

    You always say that and then it always does.

We hear the front door slam behind them. There is a short silence.

MRS DASHWOOD

    I fear Mrs Jennings is a bad influence.

She approaches ELINOR.

MRS DASHWOOD

    You must miss him, Elinor.

ELINOR looks very directly at her mother.

ELINOR

    We are not engaged, Mamma.

MRS DASHWOOD

    But he loves you, dearest, of that I am certain.

ELINOR looks down. She speaks slowly, choosing her words with care.

ELINOR

    I am by no means *assured* of his regard for me.

MRS DASHWOOD

    Oh, Elinor!

ELINOR

But even were he to feel such a . . . preference, I think we should
be foolish to assume that there would not be many obstacles to

---

his choosing a woman of no rank who cannot afford to buy sugar . . .

MRS DASHWOOD
But Elinor – your heart must tell you –

ELINOR
In such a situation, Mamma, it is perhaps better to use one's head.

She clears her throat, rises determinedly, picks up the accounts book and opens it. MRS DASHWOOD *is silenced.*

58A EXT. FIELDS NEAR BARTON COTTAGE. DAY.
MARIANNE *walks very briskly, dragging an unwilling* MARGARET *behind her.*

59 EXT. DOWNS NEAR BARTON COTTAGE. DAY.
It has started to rain. Mists are gathering around the two figures walking against the wind.

MARIANNE
Is there any felicity in the world superior to this?

MARGARET
I told you it would rain.

MARIANNE
Look! There is some blue sky! Let us chase it!

MARGARET
I'm not supposed to run . . .

MARIANNE *runs off down the hill into the heart of the mist.* MARGARET *stumbles after her, grumbling. We follow* MARIANNE *in her headlong descent and suddenly, dramatically, she trips and sprawls to the ground, letting out a sharp cry of pain.*

———

MARGARET

Marianne!

MARIANNE

Help me!

She tries to get up, but the pain in her ankle is too great. She sinks back to the ground. MARGARET is very alarmed.

MARIANNE

Margaret, run home and fetch help.

The mists have thickened. They can no longer see where they are. Despite her rising fear, MARGARET squares her shoulders bravely and tries to sense the direction.

MARGARET

I think it is this way. I will run as fast as I can, Marianne.

She dashes off. As she goes into the mist we hear the thunder of hooves. CU Margaret's terrified expression. They seem to be coming from all around. She wheels and turns and then – Crash! Through the mist breaks a huge white horse. Astride sits an Adonis in hunting gear. MARGARET squeals. The horse rears. Its rider controls it and slides off. He rushes to MARIANNE's side.

THE STRANGER

Are you hurt?

MARIANNE *(transfixed)*

Only my ankle.

THE STRANGER

May I have your permission to –

He indicates her leg. Decorous, perhaps faintly impish.

THE STRANGER

– ascertain if there are any breaks?

———

MARIANNE *nods speechlessly. With great delicacy, he feels her ankle.*
MARGARET's *eyes are out on chapel-hooks.* MARIANNE *almost swoons
with embarrassment and excitement mixed.*

THE STRANGER
It is not broken. Now, can you put your arm about my neck?

MARIANNE *does not need any encouragement. He lifts her effortlessly and
calls to his horse:* 'Bedivere!' *It trots obediently forward. The* STRANGER
smiles down at MARIANNE.

THE STRANGER
Allow me to escort you home.

60 INT. BARTON COTTAGE. DINING ROOM. DAY.
Rain is thudding against the window from which MRS DASHWOOD *turns,
looking very worried.*

MRS DASHWOOD
Marianne was sure it would not rain.

ELINOR
Which invariably means it *will*.

*But we can see she is trying to conceal her anxiety from her mother. There are
noises in the hall.*

MRS DASHWOOD
At last!

MARGARET *runs into the room dripping wet.*

MARGARET
She fell over! She fell down – and he's carrying her!

61 INT. BARTON COTTAGE. FRONT DOOR. DAY.
MRS DASHWOOD *and* ELINOR *rush to the front door. They see the*
STRANGER *carrying* MARIANNE *up the garden path, his scarlet coat
staining the monochrome rain.*

———

MRS DASHWOOD
> Marianne!

The STRANGER *reaches the door. This is no time for introductions.*

ELINOR
> In here, sir – this way. Margaret, open the door wider. Please,
> sir, lay her here. Marianne, are you in pain?

They move into the parlour.

62 INT. BARTON COTTAGE. PARLOUR. DAY.
MARIANNE *is carried in, surrounded by* ELINOR, MRS DASHWOOD
and MARGARET.

THE STRANGER
> It is a twisted ankle.

MARIANNE
> Do not be alarmed, Mamma.

The STRANGER *deposits* MARIANNE *on the sofa. They look straight into
each other's eyes. Electric.*

THE STRANGER
> I can assure you it is not serious. I took the liberty of feeling the
> bone and it is perfectly sound.

ELINOR *raises her eyebrows at* MARIANNE, *who blushes to her roots.*

MRS DASHWOOD
> Sir, I cannot even begin to thank you.

THE STRANGER
> Please do not think of it. I am honoured to be of service.

MRS DASHWOOD
> Will you not be seated?

THE STRANGER

Pray excuse me – I have no desire to leave a water mark! But permit me to call tomorrow afternoon and enquire after the patient?

MRS DASHWOOD

We shall look forward to it!

He turns to MARIANNE and smiles. She smiles back gloriously. He bows, and sweeps out of the room.

MARIANNE (*hissing*)

His name! His name!

MRS DASHWOOD silences her with a gesture and follows him out with all the solicitous charm she can command while MARGARET pokes her head around the door to watch. ELINOR is removing MARIANNE's boot and trying not to laugh at her.

63 EXT. BARTON COTTAGE. FRONT DOOR. DAY.
MRS DASHWOOD *calls out after him.*

MRS DASHWOOD

Please tell us to whom we are so much obliged?

The STRANGER mounts Bedivere and turns to her.

THE STRANGER

John Willoughby of Allenham – your servant, ma'am!

And he gallops off into the mist – we almost expect Bedivere to sprout wings. CLOSE on MRS DASHWOOD's excited expression.

64 INT. BARTON COTTAGE. PARLOUR. DAY.
MRS DASHWOOD *runs back into the parlour, jittering with excitement and anxiety.*

MARIANNE

Mr John Willoughby of Allenham!

———

54

MRS DASHWOOD

What an impressive gentleman!

MARIANNE

He lifted me as if I weighed no more than a dried leaf!

ELINOR

Is he human?

MARIANNE *hits* ELINOR. MRS DASHWOOD *tends to her ankle.*

MRS DASHWOOD

Tell me if I hurt you.

ELINOR (*regarding Marianne's ecstatic expression*)
She feels no pain, Mamma. Margaret, ask Betsy to make up a
cold compress, please.

MARGARET (*leaving reluctantly*)
Did you see him? He expressed himself well, did he not?

MRS DASHWOOD

With great decorum and honour.

MARIANNE

And spirit and wit and feeling.

ELINOR

And economy – ten words at most.

From below stairs we can hear MARGARET *wailing*

Wait for me!

MARIANNE

And he is to come tomorrow!

ELINOR

You must change, Marianne – you will catch a cold.

————

MARIANNE

What care I for colds when there is such a man?

ELINOR

You will care very much when your nose swells up.

MARIANNE

You are right. Help me, Elinor.

MARGARET *comes back with the bandages.*

MARGARET

What has happened?

ELINOR

We have decided to give you to the Gypsies.

ELINOR *and* MARIANNE *go upstairs.* MARGARET *whispers to* MRS DASHWOOD.

MARGARET

Will they be married before Edward and Elinor, do you think, Mamma?

MRS DASHWOOD

Margaret, you are worse than Mrs Jennings.

65 EXT. BARTON COTTAGE. MORNING.
The rain has cleared. SIR JOHN's *horse munches grass contentedly by the side of the road.*

SIR JOHN (V/O)

Mr Willoughby is well worth catching, Miss Dashwood – Miss Marianne must not expect to have all the men to herself!

---

66 INT. BARTON COTTAGE. PARLOUR. MORNING.

The DASHWOODS *are having a frustrating time winkling information about* WILLOUGHBY *out of* SIR JOHN, *who is in turn only anxious to protect* BRANDON's *interest.* MARIANNE *has her bandaged foot up on the sofa and is fast losing patience.*

> MARIANNE
>
> But what do you know of Mr Willoughby, Sir John?

> SIR JOHN
>
> Decent shot – and there is not a bolder rider in all England.

> MARIANNE
>
> But what is he *like*?

> SIR JOHN
>
> Like?

> MARIANNE
>
> What are his tastes? His passions? His pursuits?

> SIR JOHN (*mystified*)
>
> Well, he has the nicest little bitch of a pointer – was she out with him yesterday?

MARIANNE *gives up.* MRS DASHWOOD *takes over.*

> MRS DASHWOOD
>
> Where is Allenham, Sir John?

> SIR JOHN
>
> Nice little estate three miles east. He is to inherit it from an elderly relative – Lady Allen is her name.

Now they are getting somewhere. MARIANNE *is about to ask another question when they hear a horse galloping up. Everyone is electrified.* MARGARET *runs to the window and turns back in disappointment.*

MARGARET

It is Colonel Brandon. I shall go outside and keep watch.

MARGARET *runs out of the room.*

SIR JOHN

You are all on the lookout for Willoughby, eh? Dear me, poor Brandon. You will none of you think of him now.

BRANDON *is admitted by* BETSY. *He is carrying a large bunch of hothouse flowers.*

COLONEL BRANDON

How is the invalid?

He hands MARIANNE *the flowers with a smile.*

MARIANNE

Thank you so much, Colonel.

She rather absently hands the flowers to ELINOR, *who goes for a vase.* SIR JOHN *gestures at* BRANDON *with bluff insensitivity.*

SIR JOHN

Miss Marianne, I cannot see why you should set your cap at Mr Willoughby when you have already made such a splendid conquest!

MARIANNE

I have no intention of 'setting my cap' at anyone, Sir John!

COLONEL BRANDON

Mr Willoughby – Lady Allen's nephew?

BRANDON'*s light tone betrays no emotion.* ELINOR *comes back in with the flowers and puts them on the table next to* MARIANNE.

SIR JOHN

Aye, he visits every year for he is to inherit Allenham – and he

———

58

has a very pretty estate of his own, Miss Dashwood, Combe
Magna in Somerset. If I were you, I would not give him up to
my younger sister in spite of all this tumbling down hills . . .

*Suddenly MARGARET runs in screaming 'Marianne's preserver!' at the top
of her voice. Everyone starts to move at once. MARGARET is silenced.
BRANDON looks at MARIANNE, whose incandescent expression makes
her feelings all too clear.*

SIR JOHN
Here is the man himself. Come, Brandon – we know when we
are not wanted. Let us leave him to the ladies!

ELINOR
Marianne! Sir John and the Colonel are leaving.

MARIANNE looks up, suddenly self-conscious.

MARIANNE
Goodbye, Colonel. Thank you for the flowers.

*ELINOR sees them out. We hear WILLOUGHBY's voice outside. CLOSE on
MARIANNE's radiant anticipation.*

67 EXT. BARTON COTTAGE. FRONT DOOR. DAY.
WILLOUGHBY *is shaking hands with* COLONEL BRANDON *and* SIR
JOHN.

WILLOUGHBY
How do you do, Colonel?

SIR JOHN
How does *he* do? How do *you* do, more like. Go on in, they're
waiting for you!

*BRANDON looks at WILLOUGHBY for a moment. He bows. WIL-
LOUGHBY bows. Then BRANDON and SIR JOHN exit.*

———

68 INT. BARTON COTTAGE. PARLOUR. DAY.

ELINOR *leads in* WILLOUGHBY. MRS DASHWOOD *greets him with outstretched arms.*

> MRS DASHWOOD
>
> Mr Willoughby! What a pleasure to see you again!

> WILLOUGHBY
>
> The pleasure is all mine, I can assure you. I trust Miss Marianne has not caught cold?

> MARIANNE
>
> You have found out my name!

> WILLOUGHBY
>
> Of course. The neighbourhood is crawling with my spies.

He suddenly produces a bunch of wild flowers from behind his back and offers them to MARIANNE *with a courtly, humorous bow.*

> WILLOUGHBY
>
> And since you cannot venture out to nature, nature must be brought to you!

> MARIANNE
>
> How beautiful. *These* are not from the hothouse.

WILLOUGHBY *sees* BRANDON's *flowers.*

> WILLOUGHBY
>
> Ah! I see mine is not the first offering, nor the most elegant. I am afraid I obtained these from an obliging field.

> MARIANNE
>
> But I have always preferred wild flowers!

> WILLOUGHBY
>
> I suspected as much.

———

ELINOR *takes the delicate flowers from* WILLOUGHBY.

ELINOR
I will put these in water.

MRS DASHWOOD
Our gratitude, Mr Willoughby, is beyond expression –

WILLOUGHBY
But it is I who am grateful. I have often passed this cottage and grieved for its lonely state – and then the first news I had from Lady Allen when I arrived was that it was taken. I felt a peculiar interest in the event which nothing can account for but my present delight in meeting you.

He is merry, spirited, voluble – a breath of fresh air. ELINOR *brings back* WILLOUGHBY'*s flowers and places them next to* BRANDON'*s on the side table.*

MRS DASHWOOD
Pray sit down, Mr Willoughby.

She indicates a chair but WILLOUGHBY *sees a book lying on* MAR-IANNE'*s footstool, picks it up and – to her great delight – sits down on the stool at her feet.*

WILLOUGHBY
Who is reading Shakespeare's sonnets?

Everyone answers at once.

MARIANNE/ELINOR/MRS DASHWOOD
I am. / We all are. / Marianne.

MRS DASHWOOD
Marianne has been reading them out to us.

WILLOUGHBY
Which are your favourites?

It is a general question but MARIANNE *gaily commandeers it.*

> MARIANNE
>
> Without a doubt, mine is 116.

> WILLOUGHBY
>
> Let me not to the marriage of true minds
> Admit impediments. Love is not love
> Which alters when it alteration finds,
> Or bends with the remover to remove –
> then how does it go?

> MARIANNE
>
> 'O, no! it is an ever-fixed mark.'

WILLOUGHBY *joins in the line halfway through and continues.* ELINOR
and MRS DASHWOOD *exchange glances. Clearly, their contribution to this
conversation will be minimal.*

> WILLOUGHBY
>
> 'That looks on storms' – or is it tempests? Let me find it.

WILLOUGHBY *gets out a tiny leatherbound book.*

> WILLOUGHBY
>
> It is strange you should be reading them – for, look, I carry this
> with me always.

It is a miniature copy of the sonnets. MARIANNE *is delighted, and, mutually
astonished at this piece of synchronicity, they proceed to look up other
favourites, chatting as though they were already intimates.* MRS DASH-
WOOD *smiles at* ELINOR *with satisfaction.* ELINOR, *amused, picks up her
sewing.* MARGARET *stares.* WILLOUGHBY *and* MARIANNE *are oblivi-
ous to everything but each other.*

69 EXT. BARTON COTTAGE. GARDEN PATH. DAY.
WILLOUGHBY *is leaving. He has a flower from* MARIANNE's *bunch in his*

buttonhole and is on his horse, looking about as virile as his horse. Everyone has come out to say goodbye, MARIANNE supported by ELINOR and MRS DASHWOOD.

WILLOUGHBY

Till tomorrow! And my pocket sonnets are yours, Miss Marianne! A talisman against further injury!

MARIANNE

Goodbye! Thank you!

He gallops off. They all wave. MARGARET follows him down the road for a while.

ELINOR

Good work, Marianne! You have covered all forms of poetry; another meeting will ascertain his views on nature and romantic attachments and then you will have nothing left to talk about and the acquaintanceship will be over.

MARIANNE

I suppose I have erred against decorum. I should have been dull and spiritless and talked only of the weather, or the state of the roads . . .

ELINOR

No, but Mr Willoughby can be in no doubt of your enthusiasm for him.

MARIANNE

Why should he doubt it? Why should I hide my regard?

ELINOR

No particular reason, Marianne, only that we know so little of him –

MARIANNE

But time alone does not determine intimacy. Seven years would

---

be insufficient to make some people acquainted with each other and seven days are more than enough for others.

ELINOR

Or seven hours in this case.

MARIANNE

I feel I know Mr Willoughby well already. If I had weaker, more shallow feelings perhaps I *could* conceal them, as you do –

Then she realises what she's said.

MRS DASHWOOD

Marianne, that is not fair –

MARIANNE

I am sorry, Elinor, I did not mean . . .

ELINOR

I know. Do not trouble yourself, Marianne.

ELINOR *turns back into the house.*

MARIANNE

I do not understand her, Mamma. Why does she never mention Edward? I have never even seen her cry about him, or about Norland . . .

MRS DASHWOOD

Nor I. But Elinor is not like you or I, dear. She does not like to be swayed by her emotions.

70 INT. BARTON COTTAGE. ELINOR AND MARIANNE'S BEDROOM. DAY.
CLOSE *on Edward's handkerchief. We can see the monogram ECF clearly.* CLOSE *on* ELINOR *staring out of the window. Tears stand in her eyes but she presses the handkerchief to them before they fall.*

---

71 INT. BARTON PARK. DRAWING ROOM. EVE.

After dinner. Tea has been served. ELINOR, COLONEL BRANDON, MRS DASHWOOD *and* MRS JENNINGS *play at cards. In a far corner of the room,* MARIANNE *is concentrating as she draws a silhouette.* WILLOUGH-BY*'s profile glows behind the screen in front of her. She looks up and stops, gazing, bewitched, at his beauty. The lips move – a whisper:* Marianne. *Then, louder:* Haven't you finished? *He moves out from behind the screen, eyes full of laughter. They look at each other.*

73A INT. BARTON COTTAGE. PARLOUR. DAY.

ELINOR *and* MRS DASHWOOD *are at the accounts.* WILLOUGHBY *and* MARIANNE *are on the other side of the room in the window seat, whispering together. Clearly, he is already part of the family.*

> MRS DASHWOOD
>
> Surely you are not going to deny us beef as well as sugar?

> ELINOR
>
> There is nothing under tenpence a pound. We have to econo-mise.

> MRS DASHWOOD
>
> Do you want us to starve?

> ELINOR
>
> No. Just not to eat beef.

MRS DASHWOOD *is silenced but sighs crossly.* ELINOR *looks over to the lovers and sees* WILLOUGHBY *in the act of cutting off a lock of* MAR-IANNE*'s hair, which he kisses and places in his pocket-book.* ELINOR *is transfixed by this strangely erotic moment.* WILLOUGHBY *senses her gaze and looks over. She snaps her head back to her sums and is astonished to find that she has written 'Edward' at the top of the sheet. Hastily she rubs it out and writes 'Expenses'.*

73B EXT. BARTON CHURCH. DAY.

MRS JENNINGS *is talking to the elderly* CURATE. *Other* PARISHIONERS *exit the church as* WILLOUGHBY's *curricle (the eighteenth-century equivalent of a sports car) goes flying by.* MARIANNE *sits by his side, the picture of happiness.* MRS JENNINGS *nudges the* CURATE *and whispers. The* PARISHIONERS *stare after them and comment to each other.*

74 EXT. BARTON COTTAGE. GARDEN PATH. DAY.

MARIANNE *and* ELINOR *are coming down the path together.* MARIANNE *is dressed to go out. The argument has evidently started indoors and is being continued here.*

> MARIANNE
>
> If there was any *true* impropriety in my behaviour, I should be sensible of it, Elinor –

> ELINOR
>
> But as it has already exposed you to some very impertinent remarks, do you not begin to doubt your own discretion?

> MARIANNE
>
> If the impertinent remarks of such as Mrs Jennings are proof of impropriety, then we are all offending every moment of our lives –

The conversation is halted by the arrival of COLONEL BRANDON *on horseback.*

> COLONEL BRANDON (*dismounting*)
>
> Miss Dashwood! Miss Marianne!

> ELINOR
>
> Good morning, Colonel!

> COLONEL BRANDON
>
> I come to issue an invitation. A picnic on my estate at Delaford – if you would care to join us on Thursday next. Mrs Jennings's daughter and her husband are travelling up especially.

———

ELINOR

Thank you, Colonel, we shall be delighted.

At that moment, WILLOUGHBY's curricle hoves into view and MAR-IANNE's face lights up.

COLONEL BRANDON (*to Marianne*)

I will of course be including Mr Willoughby in the party.

Even MARIANNE is a little embarrassed and recollects her manners. She smiles kindly at BRANDON.

MARIANNE

I should be delighted to join you, Colonel!

The COLONEL helps her into the curricle, exchanging nods with WIL-LOUGHBY, who is regarding him with some suspicion.

WILLOUGHBY

Good morning, Miss Dashwood; good morning, Colonel.

MARIANNE

The Colonel has invited us to Delaford, Willoughby!

WILLOUGHBY

Excellent. I understand you have a particularly fine pianoforte, Colonel.

The undercurrents of this conversation are decidedly tense.

COLONEL BRANDON

A Broadwood Grand.

MARIANNE

A Broadwood Grand! Then I shall really be able to play for you!

WILLOUGHBY

We shall look forward to it!

———

MARIANNE *smiles her perfect happiness at him and he whips up the horses. They drive off, waving their farewells.*

BRANDON *looks after them for a silent moment, and then collects himself and turns to* ELINOR, *who is less than satisfied with their behaviour.*

> COLONEL BRANDON
> Your sister seems very happy.

> ELINOR
> Yes. Marianne does not approve of hiding her emotions. In fact, her romantic prejudices have the unfortunate tendency to set propriety at naught.

> COLONEL BRANDON
> She is wholly unspoilt.

> ELINOR
> Rather too unspoilt, in my view. The sooner she becomes acquainted with the ways of the world, the better.

COLONEL BRANDON *looks at her sharply and then speaks very deliberately, as though controlling some powerful emotion.*

> COLONEL BRANDON
> I knew a lady like your sister – the same impulsive sweetness of temper – who was forced into, as you put it, a better acquaintance with the world. The result was only ruination and despair.

He stops, and briskly remounts his horse.

> COLONEL BRANDON
> Do not desire it, Miss Dashwood.

75 EXT. BARTON PARK. DRIVE. DAY.
People and carriages fill the drive, the sun shines and the atmosphere is pleasantly expectant. SIR JOHN *is organising the provision of blankets and*

parasols and COLONEL BRANDON *is busy furnishing the* DRIVERS *with their routes. There are three new faces a pretty, blowsy* WOMAN (CHARLOTTE PALMER), *a stony-faced* MAN (MR PALMER) *and an exceedingly good-looking* GIRL (LUCY STEELE), *who are standing with* ELINOR, MARIANNE, MARGARET, MRS JENNINGS *and* MRS DASHWOOD.

MARIANNE *is standing slightly apart, looking out along the road, impatient for* WILLOUGHBY.

> #### MRS JENNINGS
> Imagine my surprise, Mrs Dashwood, when Charlotte and her lord and master appeared with our cousin Lucy! The last person I expected to see! 'Where did you pop out from, Miss?' says I. I was never so surprised to see anyone in all my life!

LUCY STEELE *smiles shyly and looks at the ground.* MRS JENNINGS *continues* sotto voce *to* MRS DASHWOOD.

> #### MRS JENNINGS
> She probably came on purpose to share the fun, for there are no funds for such luxuries at home, poor thing.

> #### LUCY
> I had not seen you for so long, dear Mrs Jennings, I could not resist the opportunity.

> #### CHARLOTTE
> Oh, you sly thing! It was the Misses Dashwood she wanted to see, not Delaford, Mamma! I have heard nothing but 'Miss Dashwood this, Miss Dashwood that' for I don't know how long! And what do you think of them now you do see them, Lucy? My mother has talked of nothing else in her letters since you came to Barton, Mrs Dashwood. Mr Palmer – are they not the very creatures she describes?

MR PALMER *regards his wife with a less than enchanted expression.*

MR PALMER
Nothing like.

CHARLOTTE (*laughing gaily*)
Why, Mr Palmer! Do you know you are quite rude today? He is to be an MP, you know, Mrs Dashwood, and it is very fatiguing for him for he is forced to make everybody like him – he says it is quite shocking –

MRS PALMER
I never said anything so irrational. Don't palm all your abuses of the language upon me.

MRS JENNINGS (*to Mrs Dashwood*)
Mr Palmer is so droll – he is always out of humour.

MR PALMER *does indeed have the air of a man under siege.* WILLOUGH-BY *suddenly appears in his curricle.* MARIANNE *waves to him with a radiant smile.* MRS JENNINGS *nudges* CHARLOTTE *and points to* MARIANNE.

MRS JENNINGS
Here he is! Now you shall see, Charlotte.

WILLOUGHBY *drives up as close to* MARIANNE *as possible, making her laugh.*

MRS JENNINGS
How now, Mr Willoughby! You must greet my daughter Charlotte, and Mr Palmer –

WILLOUGHBY
How do you do?

MRS JENNINGS
And my little cousin, Miss Lucy Steele.

———

WILLOUGHBY
Welcome to our party, Miss Steele!

LUCY *bobs demurely.* WILLOUGHBY *inclines his head politely, leaps from the curricle and hands* MARIANNE *in.* MRS JENNINGS *coos and chuckles at them.* CHARLOTTE *nudges* ELINOR.

CHARLOTTE
I know Mr Willoughby extremely well – not that I ever spoke to him but I have seen him forever in town. Your sister is monstrous lucky to get him. Mamma says Colonel Brandon is in love with her as well, which is a very great compliment for he hardly ever falls in love with anyone.

ELINOR *smiles politely.* WILLOUGHBY *moves the curricle out to the front of the drive.* CHARLOTTE *points after them and laughs with* MRS JENNINGS. LUCY *edges up beside* ELINOR.

LUCY
May I beg a seat beside you, Miss Dashwood? I have so longed to make your better acquaintance! I have heard nothing but the highest praise for you.

ELINOR *is relieved to change the subject.*

ELINOR
I would be delighted. But Sir John and Mrs Jennings are too excessive in their compliments. I am sure to disappoint.

LUCY
No, for it was from quite another source that I heard you praised and one not at all inclined to exaggeration.

LUCY *speaks in a knowing, confidential undertone, as though not wanting anyone else to hear. At that moment a* HORSEMAN *thunders up the drive towards them. Everyone turns to face the new arrival.*

———

SIR JOHN

What can this be?

It is a MESSENGER *who has obviously had a long, hard ride. He asks for* COLONEL BRANDON *and hands him a letter, which* BRANDON *tears open.* MRS JENNINGS *is puce with suppressed curiosity.*

COLONEL BRANDON

My horse! Quickly!

SIR JOHN

What is the matter, Brandon?

COLONEL BRANDON

I must away to London.

SIR JOHN

No! Impossible!

Everyone gathers round BRANDON, *who is, naturally, mortified. A* SERVANT *brings up the* COLONEL's *horse.*

COLONEL BRANDON

Imperative.

There is a murmur of disappointment from the party. SIR JOHN *is embarrassed and protests again.*

SIR JOHN

But Brandon, we are all assembled. We cannot picnic at Delaford without our host! Go up to town tomorrow.

WILLOUGHBY

Or wait till we return and start then – you would not be six hours later.

COLONEL BRANDON

I cannot afford to lose one minute.

———

As he speaks, he is mounting his horse. His grave urgency silences all protest and he gallops off, leaving everyone stunned and, of course, deeply curious. Then they all start to talk at once. LUCY is still next to ELINOR.

LUCY
Oh, Miss Dashwood, I cannot bear it! Just when I was to have the opportunity of speaking with you.

76 EXT. MEADOW NEAR BARTON COTTAGE. DAY.
Having been denied their trip, the DASHWOODS and WILLOUGHBY have set out an impromptu picnic. WILLOUGHBY is wandering restlessly about. The weather is sublime.

WILLOUGHBY
Frailty, thy name is Brandon!

MARIANNE
There are some people who cannot bear a party of pleasure. I think he wrote the letter himself as a trick for getting out of it.

MRS DASHWOOD (*indulgently*)
You are a very wicked pair, Colonel Brandon will be sadly missed.

WILLOUGHBY
Why? When he is the kind of man that everyone speaks well of and no one wants to talk to.

MARIANNE
Exactly!

ELINOR
Nonsense.

MRS DASHWOOD
Colonel Brandon is very highly esteemed at the Park.

73

WILLOUGHBY
Which is enough censure in itself.

ELINOR (*half laughing*)
Really, Willoughby!

WILLOUGHBY (*imitating Mrs Jennings perfectly*)
Come, come, Mr Impudence – I know you and your wicked ways – oh!

He gives a little shriek and waddles about the garden doing her walk. He comes up to ELINOR *and puts his head on her shoulder.*

WILLOUGHBY
Come, Miss Dashwood, reveal your beau, reveal him, I say! Let's have no secrets between friends! Let me winkle them out of you!

ELINOR *hits him on the nose with her teaspoon and he waddles off to* MARIANNE.

WILLOUGHBY (*as Mrs Jennings*)
I declare, Miss Marianne, if I do not have you married to the Colonel by teatime, I shall swallow my own bonnet.

MARIANNE *laughs.* WILLOUGHBY *drops the parody suddenly.*

WILLOUGHBY
As if you *could* marry such a character.

ELINOR
Why should you dislike him?

There is indeed an edge to WILLOUGHBY's *raillery. He flicks* ELINOR *an almost alarmed glance and then sweeps* MARIANNE *to her feet and starts to dance around the garden with her.*

WILLOUGHBY
Because he has threatened me with rain when I wanted it fine,

---

he has found fault with the balance of my curricle and I cannot persuade him to buy my brown mare. If it will be of any satisfaction to you, however, to be told I believe his character to be in all other respects irreproachable, I am ready to confess it. And in return for an acknowledgement that must give me some pain (*he is slowing down*) you cannot deny me the privilege (*slower still*) of disliking *him* (*and stopping*) as much as I *adore* –

He and MARIANNE are standing looking at each other. The expression on WILLOUGHBY's face is heart-stopping. MARGARET has stopped eating and is staring with her mouth open.

ELINOR glances at MRS DASHWOOD but she is gazing up at them with almost as many stars in her eyes as MARIANNE.

Suddenly WILLOUGHBY breaks the mood by swinging away from MARIANNE and gesturing to the house.

WILLOUGHBY
– this cottage!

The tension is broken. MARGARET starts to chew again.

MRS DASHWOOD
I have great plans for improvements to it, you know, Mr Willoughby.

WILLOUGHBY
Now *that* I will never consent to. Not a stone must be added to its walls. Were I rich enough, I would instantly pull down Combe Magna and build it up again in the exact image of that cottage!

ELINOR
With dark, narrow stairs, a poky hall and a fire that smokes?

WILLOUGHBY

Especially the fire that smokes! Then I might be as happy at Combe Magna as I have been at Barton.

He looks at MARIANNE, *who has gone to sit at her mother's feet.*

WILLOUGHBY

But this place has one claim on my affection which no other can possibly share.

MARIANNE *is so irradiated with happiness that she looks like an angel.*

WILLOUGHBY

Promise me you will never change it.

MRS DASHWOOD

I do not have the heart.

ELINOR

Or the money.

77 EXT. BARTON COTTAGE. GARDEN PATH AND GATE. DUSK.
MARIANNE *is seeing* WILLOUGHBY *off.*

WILLOUGHBY

Miss Marianne, will you – will you do me the honour of granting me an interview tomorrow – alone?

MARIANNE

Willoughby, we are always alone!

WILLOUGHBY

But there is something very particular I should like to ask you.

There is something about his formal tone that makes her feel shy.

MARIANNE

Of course. I shall ask Mamma if I may stay behind from church.

WILLOUGHBY
Thank you. Until tomorrow then – Miss Marianne.

He mounts Bedivere and leaves. MARIANNE looks after him, her eyes shining. He is coming to propose.

78 EXT. LONDON TENEMENTS. NIGHT.
A district of extreme poverty, populated by the LOWLIFE of LONDON: FOOTPADS, dogs, rats and SCAVENGERS of all kinds. In the distance a tavern belches forth drunken REVELLERS who sway and reel into the night. A hooded HORSEMAN pulls up his exhausted steed at the entrance to a slum. He dismounts and looks up at one of the windows. The rags hanging there twitch as if someone is watching for him. He strides inside.

79 INT. TENEMENT STAIRS. NIGHT.
Stepping over a supine BEGGAR at the foot of the stairs, the HORSEMAN flings back his hood – it is BRANDON, hollow-eyed and dropping with weariness. We follow him up the stairs to a door which is opened by an OLDER WOMAN.

80 INT. TENEMENT ROOM. NIGHT.
He enters a bare room partitioned with filthy rags hung from the ceiling and lit with stinking tallow lamps. At the window stands the slight figure of a VERY YOUNG WOMAN. She turns. BRANDON reacts with a tender smile which stiffens into an expression of deep shock. We see her silhouette. She is heavily pregnant. She bursts into tears and runs into his arms.

81 INT. BARTON CHURCH. DAY.
Amongst the small CONGREGATION listening to the sermon drone on, we see the excited faces of ELINOR, MARGARET and MRS DASHWOOD.

MARGARET
Do you think he will kneel down when he asks her?

ELINOR
Shhh!

———

MARGARET (*with satisfaction*)
They always kneel down.

82 EXT. BARTON COTTAGE. GARDEN PATH. DAY.
The DASHWOODS *return from church to find* THOMAS *grooming*
Bedivere at the garden gate. Their excitement mounts.

83 INT. BARTON COTTAGE. FRONT DOOR. DAY.
They all enter the cottage, talking nonsense loudly in order to signal their
presence. MARGARET *giggles. Suddenly,* MARIANNE *bursts out of the*
parlour sobbing, and disappears into the room opposite. ELINOR *and*
MARGARET *stand by the door in utter consternation, while* MRS DASH-
WOOD *goes to* MARIANNE.

MRS DASHWOOD
What is wrong, my dearest?

MARIANNE *shakes her head and waves them away.*

84 INT. BARTON COTTAGE. PARLOUR. DAY.
ELINOR, MARGARET *and* MRS DASHWOOD *enter to find* WIL-
LOUGHBY *standing in a frozen attitude by the fireplace.*

MRS DASHWOOD
Willoughby! What is the matter?

WILLOUGHBY
I – forgive me, Mrs Dashwood. I am sent – that is to say, Lady
Allen has exercised the privilege of riches upon a dependent
cousin and is sending me to London.

He cannot look any of them in the eye.

MRS DASHWOOD
When – this morning?

WILLOUGHBY
Almost this moment.

MRS DASHWOOD
How very disappointing! But your business will not detain you from us for long, I hope?

WILLOUGHBY
You are very kind – but I have no idea of returning immediately to Devonshire. I am seldom invited to Allenham more than once a year.

MRS DASHWOOD
For shame, Willoughby! Can you wait for an invitation from Barton Cottage?

WILLOUGHBY
My engagements at present are of such a nature – that is – I dare not flatter myself –

The atmosphere is thick with tension. WILLOUGHBY *flicks a glance at the three* WOMEN *staring at him in mute astonishment.*

WILLOUGHBY
It is folly to linger in this manner. I will not torment myself further.

He rushes past them and out of the cottage. They follow him to the door.

85 EXT. BARTON COTTAGE. FRONT DOOR. DAY.
The DASHWOODS *cluster round the door.*

MARGARET
Willoughby, come back!

She is silenced by ELINOR *as* WILLOUGHBY *seizes Bedivere's reins from* THOMAS, *mounts up and rides off at a furious pace.*

86 INT. BARTON COTTAGE. PARLOUR. DAY.
They all rush back into the parlour.

ELINOR

Meg, dearest, please ask Betsy to make a cup of hot tea for Marianne.

MARGARET *nods dumbly and goes.* MRS DASHWOOD *has her arms around* MARIANNE.

MRS DASHWOOD

What is wrong, my love?

MARIANNE

Nothing! Please do not ask me questions!

MARIANNE *struggles free.*

MARIANNE

Please let me be!

She runs off upstairs and we hear her bedroom door slamming. There is a moment of stunned silence.

ELINOR

They must have quarrelled.

MRS DASHWOOD

That is unlikely. Perhaps this – Lady Allen – disapproves of his regard for Marianne and has invented an excuse to send him away?

ELINOR

Then why did he not say as much? It is not like Willoughby to be secretive. Did he think Marianne was richer than she is?

MRS DASHWOOD

How could he?

She gestures to the room and then looks at ELINOR *with a frown.*

MRS DASHWOOD

What is it you suspect him of?

ELINOR

I can hardly tell you. But why was his manner so guilty?

MRS DASHWOOD

What are you saying, Elinor? That he has been acting a part to your sister for all this time?

MRS DASHWOOD *is getting defensive.* ELINOR *pauses to think.*

ELINOR

No, he loves her, I am sure.

MRS DASHWOOD

Of course he loves her!

ELINOR

But has he left her with any assurance of his return? Cannot you ask her if he has proposed?

MRS DASHWOOD

Certainly not. I cannot force a confidence from Marianne and nor must you. We must trust her to confide in us in her own time.

ELINOR (*shaking her head*)

There was something so underhand in the manner of his leaving.

MRS DASHWOOD

You are resolved, then, to think the worst of him.

ELINOR

Not resolved –

MRS DASHWOOD (*cold*)

I prefer to give him the benefit of my good opinion. He deserves no less. From all of us.

She stalks out of the room and starts up the stairs. ELINOR follows her.

ELINOR

Mamma, I am very fond of Willoughby –

MRS DASHWOOD goes into her bedroom and shuts the door. ELINOR is halfway up the stairs. She meets a wet-eyed MARGARET coming down with a cup of tea.

MARGARET

She would not let me in.

ELINOR takes the cup and MARGARET runs out into the garden in tears. The sound of sobbing also comes from MARIANNE's room, and now from MRS DASHWOOD's as well. ELINOR sits down helplessly on the stairs and drinks the tea.

87 EXT. BARTON COTTAGE. RAIN. DAY.
The rain has settled in. The cottage looks cold and bleak.

88 INT. BARTON COTTAGE. UPSTAIRS CORRIDOR. DAY.
BETSY carries another uneaten meal from MARIANNE's room. She looks at the food and tuts in anxiety.

89 INT. BARTON COTTAGE. ELINOR AND MARIANNE'S BEDROOM. DAY.
MARIANNE is sitting by the window looking out at the rain through tear-swollen eyes. WILLOUGHBY's sonnets are on her lap.

MARIANNE

How like a winter hath my absence been
From thee, the pleasure of the fleeting year!
What freezings have I felt, what dark days seen!
What old December's bareness everywhere!

91 EXT. BARTON PARK. RAIN. EVE.
Smoke issues from every chimney in the place.

---

92 INT. BARTON PARK. DRAWING ROOM. EVE.

Dinner is over. MARIANNE sits listlessly by the window. MR PALMER is hiding behind a newspaper. SIR JOHN and MARGARET are looking at a map and discussing routes through China. LUCY, CHARLOTTE, MRS DASHWOOD and MRS JENNINGS are at cards. ELINOR is reading.

CHARLOTTE

Oh! If only this rain would stop!

MR PALMER (*from behind the paper*)

If only *you* would stop.

MRS JENNINGS *and* CHARLOTTE *laugh at him.*

MRS JENNINGS

'Twas you took her off my hands, Mr Palmer, and a very good bargain you made of it too, but now I have the whip hand over you for you cannot give her back!

The heavy silence behind the paper attests to the unhappy truth of this statement.

MRS JENNINGS

Miss Marianne, come and play a round with us! Looking out at the weather will not bring him back.

CHARLOTTE (*sotto voce*)

She ate nothing at dinner.

MRS JENNINGS

Mind, we are all a little forlorn these days. London has swallowed all our company.

CHARLOTTE *and* MRS JENNINGS *start to gossip about the disappearances of* BRANDON *and* WILLOUGHBY. *LUCY walks over and sits by* ELINOR, *who politely puts aside the book.*

LUCY (*low*)

Dear Miss Dashwood, perhaps now we might have our – discussion . . .

ELINOR

Our discussion?

LUCY *looks around at MRS JENNINGS and lowers her voice still further, so that ELINOR is obliged to move her chair nearer.*

LUCY

There is a particular question I have long wanted to ask you, but perhaps you will think me impertinent?

ELINOR

I cannot imagine so.

LUCY

But it is an odd question. Forgive me, I have no wish to trouble you –

She looks away coyly as if deciding whether to speak.

ELINOR

My dear Miss Steele –

CHARLOTTE (*interrupting*)

Miss Dashwood, if only Mr Willoughby had gone home to Combe Magna, we could have taken Miss Marianne to see him! For we live but half a mile away.

MR PALMER

Five and a half.

CHARLOTTE

No, I cannot believe it is that far, for you can see the place from the top of our hill. Is it really five and a half miles? No! I cannot believe it.

———

MR PALMER

Try.

ELINOR

You have my permission to ask any manner of question, if that is of any help.

LUCY

Thank you. I wonder, are you at all acquainted with your sister-in-law's mother? Mrs Ferrars?

ELINOR *sits back in deep surprise.*

ELINOR

With Fanny's mother? No, I have never met her.

LUCY

I am sure you think me strange for enquiring – if I dared tell –

MRS JENNINGS (*shouting over*)

If she tells you aught of the famous 'Mr F', Lucy, you are to pass it on.

ELINOR *tries to ignore* MRS JENNINGS, *who is keeping a curious eye on them.*

LUCY

Will you take a turn with me, Miss Dashwood?

LUCY *rises and takes* ELINOR's *arm. She guides her as far away as possible from* MRS JENNINGS *and* CHARLOTTE.

ELINOR

I had no idea at all that you were connected with that family.

LUCY

Oh! I am certainly nothing to Mrs Ferrars at present – but the time may come when we may be very *intimately* connected.

ELINOR (*low*)

What do you mean? Do you have an understanding with Fanny's brother Robert?

LUCY

The youngest? No, I never saw him in my life. No, with Edward.

ELINOR

Edward?

ELINOR *stops walking.*

ELINOR

Edward Ferrars?

LUCY *nods.*

LUCY

Edward and I have been secretly engaged these five years.

ELINOR *is frozen to the spot.*

LUCY

You may well be surprised. I should never have mentioned it, had I not known I could entirely trust you to keep our secret. Edward cannot mind me telling you for he looks on you quite as his own sister.

ELINOR *walks on mechanically. Disbelief has set in.*

ELINOR

I am sorry, but we surely – we cannot mean the same Mr Ferrars?

LUCY

The very same – he was four years under the tutelage of my uncle Mr Pratt, down in Plymouth. Has he never spoken of it?

ELINOR (*awareness dawning*)
Mr Pratt! Yes, I believe he has . . .

———

LUCY

I was very unwilling to enter into it without his mother's approval but we loved each other with too great a passion for prudence. Though you do not know him so well as I, Miss Dashwood, you must have seen how capable he is of making a woman sincerely attached to him. I cannot pretend it has not been very hard on us both. We can hardly meet above twice a year.

She sniffs and produces a large handkerchief which she holds to her eyes so that the monogram is clearly visible. ECF. ELINOR, seeing the copy of the handkerchief she has held so dear, moves quickly to a chair and sits down.

LUCY

You seem out of sorts, Miss Dashwood – are you quite well?

ELINOR

Perfectly well, thank you.

LUCY

I have not offended you?

ELINOR

On the contrary.

MRS JENNINGS *has been watching. Now she rises, unable to contain herself.*

MRS JENNINGS

I can stand it no longer, I must know what you are saying, Lucy! Miss Dashwood is quite engrossed!

MRS JENNINGS *starts to bear down on them.* LUCY *whispers with real urgency.*

LUCY

Oh, Miss Dashwood, if anyone finds out, it will ruin him – you

———

must not tell a soul! Edward says you would not break your word to save your life! Promise me!

ECU *on* ELINOR's *face.*

ELINOR
I give you my word.

MRS JENNINGS *looms over them.*

MRS JENNINGS
Well, what can have fascinated you to such an extent, Miss Dashwood?

CHARLOTTE
Tell us all!

ELINOR *cannot speak but* LUCY *glides smoothly in.*

LUCY
We were talking of London, ma'am, and all its – diversions.

MRS JENNINGS
Do you hear, Charlotte?

MRS JENNINGS *claps her hands delightedly.*

MRS JENNINGS
While you were so busy whispering, Charlotte and I have concocted a plan!

CHARLOTTE
It is the best plan in the world.

MRS JENNINGS
I make for London shortly and I invite you, Lucy, and both the Misses Dashwood to join me!

ELINOR *cannot hide her dismay.* MARIANNE *springs from her seat.*

MARIANNE

London!

MARGARET

Oh, can I go! Can *I* go?

MRS DASHWOOD

You know perfectly well you are too young, dearest.

MRS JENNINGS

I shall convey you all to my house in Berkeley Street and we shall taste all the delights of the season – what say you?

MARGARET

Oh, *please* can I go? I'm twelve soon.

CHARLOTTE

Mr Palmer, do you not long to have the Misses Dashwood come to London?

MR PALMER

I came into Devonshire with no other view.

ELINOR *exerts herself.*

ELINOR

Mrs Jennings, you are very kind, but we cannot possibly leave our mother . . .

LUCY'*s calculating eyes turn to* MRS DASHWOOD *with alacrity.*

LUCY

Indeed, the loss would be too great.

A chorus of objections goes up, particularly from MRS DASHWOOD, *who is both delighted and relieved to see* MARIANNE *with a smile on her face.*

————

MRS JENNINGS

Your mother can spare you very well.

MRS DASHWOOD

Of course I can!

CHARLOTTE

Of course she can!

SIR JOHN

And look at Miss Marianne – it would break her heart to deny
her!

MRS JENNINGS

I will brook no refusal, Miss Dashwood!

MARIANNE *claps her hands, her eyes ablaze with joy.* MRS JENNINGS
takes ELINOR's *hand.*

MRS JENNINGS

Let you and me strike hands upon the bargain – and if I do not
have the three of you married by Michaelmas, it will not be my
fault!

93 INT. BARTON COTTAGE. ELINOR/MARIANNE'S BEDROOM.
NIGHT.

We are in ELINOR *and* MARIANNE's *bedroom.* ELINOR *is in bed. She is
lying on her side with her back to* MARIANNE. *We are* CLOSE *on her face.*
MARIANNE *is running around excitedly, pulling out ribbons, looking at
dresses, etc.*

MARIANNE

I was never so grateful in all my life as I am to Mrs Jennings.
What a kind woman she is! I like her more than I can say. Oh,
Elinor! I shall see Willoughby. Think how surprised he will be!
And you will see Edward!

———

ELINOR *cannot reply.*

MARIANNE
Are you asleep?

ELINOR
With you in the room?

MARIANNE *laughs.*

MARIANNE
I do *not* believe you feel as calm as you look, not even you, Elinor. I will never sleep tonight! Oh, what were you and Miss Steele whispering about so long?

CLOSE *on* ELINOR's *expression as she struggles with the impossibility of unburdening herself to her sister without breaking her promise to* LUCY. *After a pause –*

ELINOR
Nothing of significance.

MARIANNE *looks at* ELINOR *curiously, then returns to her packing.*

95 EXT. BARTON COTTAGE. GARDEN GATE. DAY.
MRS DASHWOOD *and* MARGARET *are waving* MRS JENNINGS's *carriage off.* MARIANNE *waves back with such exuberance that she practically falls out.*

96 INT. MRS JENNINGS'S CARRIAGE. ROAD TO LONDON. DAY.
MRS JENNINGS *is chattering about London to* MARIANNE, *who listens with new-found tolerance.* LUCY *is whispering into* ELINOR's *ear.*

LUCY
I have written to Edward, Miss Dashwood, and yet I do not know how much I may see of him. Secrecy is vital – he will never be able to call.

———

ELINOR

I should imagine not.

LUCY

It is so hard. I believe my only comfort has been the constancy of his affection.

ELINOR

You are fortunate, over such a lengthy engagement, never to have had any doubts on that score.

LUCY *looks at* ELINOR *sharply, but* ELINOR *is impassive.*

LUCY

Oh! I am of rather a jealous nature and if he had talked more of one young lady than any other . . . but he has never given a moment's alarm on that count.

We can see from ELINOR's *expression that she understands* LUCY *perfectly. The strain around her eyes is pronounced.*

LUCY

Imagine how glad he will be to learn that we are friends!

97A EXT. LONDON STREET. DAY.
MRS JENNINGS's *carriage trundles along.*

98 EXT. MRS JENNINGS'S HOUSE. LONDON. DAY.
Establishing shot of a handsome town house. MRS JENNINGS's *carriage comes into shot and stops in front of it.*

99 INT. MRS JENNINGS'S HOUSE. HALL. DAY.
They enter the grand hallway under the supercilious gaze of a powdered FOOTMAN (MR PIGEON). ELINOR *is haggard after two days of close proximity with* LUCY. MRS JENNINGS *is all officious bustle and* MAR-IANNE *is feverish with anticipation. She whispers to* MRS JENNINGS, *who laughs heartily.*

———

MRS JENNINGS

To be sure, my dear, you must just hand it to Pigeon there. He will take care of it.

MARIANNE *hands a letter to the sphinxlike* FOOTMAN. *We can see a large W in the address.* ELINOR *looks at* MARIANNE *enquiringly but* MARIANNE *moves away from her.*

MRS JENNINGS

Lord above, you do not waste any time, Miss Marianne!

MARIANNE *glances self-consciously at* ELINOR *and follows* MRS JENNINGS *upstairs.* LUCY *goes up to* ELINOR *and whispers.*

LUCY

A letter! So they are definitely engaged! Mrs Jennings says your sister will buy her wedding clothes here in town.

ELINOR

Indeed Miss Steele, I know of no such plan.

But ELINOR *does not know what else to say. She marches firmly upstairs.*

100 INT. MRS JENNINGS'S HOUSE. DRAWING ROOM. DAY.
MARIANNE *and* ELINOR *have changed from their travelling clothes and are having a cup of tea. At least,* ELINOR *is.* MARIANNE *is pacing up and down in front of the window.*

ELINOR

John and Fanny are in town. I think we shall be forced to see them.

There is a faint knocking from somewhere. MARIANNE *jumps.*

ELINOR

I think it was for next door.

MARIANNE *looks out of the window.*

———

MARIANNE

Yes, you are right.

She sits down with a rueful smile. Suddenly a much louder rap is heard and they both jump. We hear a bustling downstairs. MARIANNE can hardly breathe. She goes to the drawing-room door, opens it, goes out, comes back in. We hear a MAN's voice.

MARIANNE

Oh, Elinor! It is Willoughby, indeed it is!

She turns and almost throws herself into the arms of COLONEL BRANDON.

MARIANNE

Oh! Excuse me, Colonel –

She leaves the room hastily. ELINOR *is so ashamed of* MARIANNE's *rudeness that she does not at first notice* BRANDON's *mood of tense distress.*

ELINOR

Colonel Brandon, what a pleasure to see you! Have you been in London all this while?

COLONEL BRANDON

I have. How is your dear mother?

ELINOR

Very well, thank you.

Silence.

ELINOR

Colonel, is there anything –

But BRANDON *interrupts her.*

94

COLONEL BRANDON

Forgive me, Miss Dashwood, but I have heard reports through town . . . is it impossible to – but I could have no chance of succeeding – indeed I hardly know what to do. Tell me once and for all, is everything finally resolved between your sister and Mr Willoughby?

ELINOR *is torn between discomfiture and compassion.*

ELINOR

Colonel, though neither one has informed me of their under-standing, I have no doubt of their mutual affection.

BRANDON *stands very still.*

COLONEL BRANDON

Thank you, Miss Dashwood. To your sister I wish all imagin-able happiness. To Mr Willoughby, that he . . . may endeavour to deserve her.

His tone is heavy with some bitter meaning.

ELINOR

What do you mean?

But he recollects himself.

COLONEL BRANDON

Forgive me, I – forgive me.

He bows and leaves abruptly. ELINOR *is deeply troubled.*

101 EXT. GREENWICH ARCADE. LONDON. DAY.
The PALMERS, MRS JENNINGS, JOHN, FANNY, LUCY, ELINOR *and* MARIANNE *are walking through the arcade. Additional wealth has evidently encouraged* FANNY *sartorially and she sprouts as much fruit and feathers as a market stall.* LUCY *is holding* ELINOR's *arm in a pinionlike grip.* MRS JENNINGS *is gossiping with* CHARLOTTE. MAR-

.

IANNE's good looks are heightened by her feverish expectation of seeing
WILLOUGHBY at every step, and many young men raise their hats to her
and turn as she passes.

MARIANNE
Where is dear Edward, John? We expect to see him daily.

FANNY stiffens. LUCY's sharp eyes dart hither and thither. MRS JEN-
NINGS senses gossip. ELINOR steels herself.

MRS JENNINGS
And who is 'dear Edward'?

CHARLOTTE
Who indeed?

FANNY smiles glacially.

FANNY
My brother, Mrs Jennings – Edward Ferrars.

MRS JENNINGS looks at ELINOR in sly triumph.

MRS JENNINGS
Indeed! Is that Ferrars with an F?

She and CHARLOTTE chuckle to each other. LUCY looks at ELINOR.

102 INT. MRS JENNINGS'S HOUSE. HALL. EVE.
MRS JENNINGS, LUCY, ELINOR and MARIANNE return from their
outing. MARIANNE immediately assails PIGEON.

MARIANNE
Are there any messages, Pigeon?

PIGEON
No, ma'am.

MARIANNE
No message at all? No cards?

PIGEON (*affronted*)

    None, ma'am.

MARIANNE *sighs with disappointment and starts up the stairs.* MRS JENNINGS *looks archly at* ELINOR.

MRS JENNINGS

    I note you do not enquire for *your* messages, Miss Dashwood!

ELINOR

    No, for I do not expect any, Mrs Jennings. I have very little acquaintance in town.

And she follows MARIANNE *firmly upstairs.* LUCY *watches her go, and* MRS JENNINGS *chuckles and turns to her.*

MRS JENNINGS

    She is as sly as you, Lucy!

103 INT. MRS JENNINGS'S HOUSE. BEDROOM. NIGHT.
ELINOR *wakes up. The flickering of a candle has disturbed her. She sits up in bed and sees* MARIANNE *sitting at the desk in her nightgown, writing another letter.*

ELINOR

    Marianne, is anything wrong?

MARIANNE

    Nothing at all. Go back to sleep.

104 INT. MRS JENNINGS'S HOUSE. MORNING ROOM. NIGHT.
MARIANNE, *in her nightclothes and dressing gown, paces restlessly, her letter in her hands. A slight knock at the door heralds a much-ruffled* PIGEON, *wig askew.* MARIANNE *hands him the letter. He bows and goes, highly disgruntled.*

----

105 INT. MRS JENNINGS'S HOUSE. HALL. MORNING.

MRS JENNINGS *is giving* PIGEON *his instructions for the day.* MAR-IANNE *comes running downstairs.* PIGEON *regards her drily.*

> PIGEON
> No messages, ma'am.

MARIANNE *looks so dejected that* MRS JENNINGS *takes her hand.*

> MRS JENNINGS
> Do not fret, my dear. I am told that this good weather is keeping many sportsmen in the country at present, but the frost will drive them back to town very soon, depend upon it.

MARIANNE *brightens.*

> MARIANNE
> Of course! I had not thought of – thank you, Mrs Jennings!

She runs back upstairs. MRS JENNINGS *calls after her.*

> MRS JENNINGS
> And Miss Dashwood may set her heart at rest, for I overheard your sister-in-law say that she was to bring the elusive Mr F to the ball tonight!

106 EXT. GRAND CRESCENT LEADING TO BALLROOM ENTRANCE. NIGHT.

So many carriages have entered the crescent to deliver the GUESTS *that gridlock has occurred and people are forced to walk to the entrance. We see* MRS JENNINGS, MARIANNE, ELINOR *and* LUCY *alighting from their carriage and picking their way through the mud, their skirts raised above their ankles.* ELINOR *nearly trips and is obliged to grab onto* LUCY *in order not to slip into the dirt.*

107 INT. GRAND BALLROOM. EVE.

The great ballroom is crammed with GUESTS *all determined to enjoy themselves despite the considerable inconveniences caused by noise, heat and overcrowding. MEN are sweating profusely, WOMEN dab their brows, rack punch is being swallowed by the gallon, flirting is conducted at fever pitch and all conversation is inordinately loud. Only the DANCERS have a modicum of space in which to perform their mincing steps. MRS JEN-NINGS and her brood bump into the PALMERS.*

CHARLOTTE (*screeching*)
This is very merry!

MRS JENNINGS *then spots FANNY, who is conducting a desultory conversation with an overpowdered ACQUAINTANCE. She drags ELI-NOR, MARIANNE and LUCY over to her.*

MRS JENNINGS
There you are! Goodness, how hot it is, Mrs Dashwood. You are not alone, I trust?

FANNY
Indeed not. John is just gone to fetch my brother – he has been eating ices.

LUCY *clutches at ELINOR's sleeve.*

MRS JENNINGS
Your brother! I declare, that is good news indeed. At long last!

And she beams her approval upon ELINOR.

LUCY (*whispering*)
Miss Dashwood, I declare I shall faint clean away.

FANNY *has seen JOHN threading his way towards them and waves at him. There is someone behind him. LUCY preens. JOHN bows to them.*

JOHN
Mrs Jennings, may I present my brother-in-law?

He turns to reveal a good-looking young MAN with a vacuous smile.

———

JOHN

Mr Robert Ferrars!

ROBERT

My dear ladies – we meet at last!

There is a general bowing and shaking of hands. ELINOR *is relieved.* LUCY *drops a low curtsy.*

MRS JENNINGS

So you must be the younger brother? Is Mr Edward not here? Miss Dashwood here was counting on him!

ROBERT *looks* ELINOR *up and down. He exchanges glances with* FANNY *before he speaks.*

ROBERT

Oh! He is far too busy for such gatherings – and has no special acquaintance here to make his attendance worthwhile.

MRS JENNINGS *looks at* ELINOR *in puzzlement.*

MRS JENNINGS

Well, I declare, I do not know what the young men are about these days – are they all in hiding?

ELINOR *looks down, agonised with embarrassment.*

MRS JENNINGS

Come, Mr Robert, in the absence of your brother, *you* must dance with our lovely Miss Dashwood!

ROBERT (*not best pleased*)

It would be my honour.

He turns to LUCY *and bows.*

ROBERT

And perhaps Miss Steele might consider reserving the allemande?

LUCY *curtsies again.* ROBERT *escorts a most unwilling* ELINOR *onto the dance floor.*

ROBERT
You reside in Devonshire, I b'lieve, Miss Dashwood?

ELINOR
We do.

ROBERT
In a cottage?

ELINOR
Yes.

ROBERT
I am excessively fond of a cottage. If I had any money to spare, I should build one myself.

Luckily for ELINOR *the set changes and she is obliged to turn away from* ROBERT. *She wheels round to face her new partner. It is* WILLOUGHBY! *They both stop dancing and stare at each other aghast. A traffic jam starts and they are forced to take hands and resume the steps.*

WILLOUGHBY (*stiff*)
How do you do, Miss Dashwood?

ELINOR *does not know quite how to respond.*

ELINOR
I am well, thank you, Mr Willoughby.

She looks about for MARIANNE, *instinctively wanting to keep her away from* WILLOUGHBY.

WILLOUGHBY
How is your – family?

———

ELINOR (*cold*)
We are all extremely well, Mr Willoughby – thank you for your
kind enquiry.

WILLOUGHBY *is shamed into silence. Then he sees* MARIANNE. *At the
same moment the music pauses.* MARIANNE *looks up. In the brief moment
of relative quiet, her great cry rings across the room.*

MARIANNE
Willoughby!

Everyone turns to look as MARIANNE *rushes towards him with both arms
outstretched, her face luminous with joy. As the noise of the room builds
again and* PEOPLE *change their partners, we are aware that many are
surreptitiously watching.* MARIANNE *reaches him but* WILLOUGHBY
stands with his arms frozen at his side. MARIANNE *gives a little confused
laugh.*

MARIANNE
Good God, Willoughby! Will you not shake hands with me?

WILLOUGHBY *looks extremely uncomfortable and glances towards a
group of very smart* PEOPLE *who are watching him closely. Central to
this group is a* SOPHISTICATED WOMAN *who frowns at him proprietorially.*

WILLOUGHBY *shakes* MARIANNE's *hand briefly. Behind her,* MRS
JENNINGS *is giving an animated commentary to* FANNY *and* JOHN,
while LUCY *whispers in* ROBERT's *ear as they go past to join the set.*

WILLOUGHBY (*strangled*)
How do you do, Miss Marianne?

MARIANNE
Willoughby, what is the matter? Why have you not come to see
me? Were you not in London? Have you not received my letters?

WILLOUGHBY *is sweating with tension.*

> ### WILLOUGHBY
> Yes, I had the pleasure of receiving the information which you were so good as to send me.

> ### MARIANNE (*piteously*)
> For heaven's sake, Willoughby, tell me what is wrong!

> ### WILLOUGHBY
> Thank you – I am most obliged. If you will excuse me, I must return to my party.

He bows, white to the teeth, and walks away to join the SOPHISTICATED WOMAN.

> ### MARIANNE
> Willoughby!

He is drawn away by his PARTY, *some of whom look back at* MARIANNE *with a mixture of curiosity and condescension.* MARIANNE *almost sinks to her knees.* ELINOR *supports her.*

> ### ELINOR
> Marianne! Come away!

> ### MARIANNE
> Go to him, Elinor – force him to come to me.

MRS JENNINGS *has come up, full of concern.*

> ### ELINOR
> Dearest, do not betray what you feel to everyone present! This is not the place for explanations –

> ### MRS JENNINGS
> Come along, dear.

They almost have to drag MARIANNE *away.* MRS JENNINGS *turns back to the* DASHWOOD *party.* FANNY *and* JOHN *have practically imploded*

*with embarrassment and are distancing themselves as much as possible from
the source. LUCY and ROBERT are dancing nearby.*

> MRS JENNINGS
> Will you come, Lucy?

> LUCY
> Oh, are we leaving so soon?

> ROBERT
> If I might be so bold, Mrs Jennings, it would be our pleasure to
> escort your young charge home.

> LUCY
> How very kind!

> MRS JENNINGS
> That is very handsome –

*She rushes off to follow MARIANNE and ELINOR. We stay for a moment
with LUCY and ROBERT who have left the set.*

> ROBERT
> She actually sent him messages during the night?

*CAM rises to show the DASHWOODS exiting past the whispering, sneering
faces of the CROWD.*

108 INT. MRS JENNINGS'S HOUSE. BEDROOM. NIGHT.
MARIANNE *sits scribbling a letter at the desk.*

> ELINOR
> Marianne, please tell me –

> MARIANNE
> Do not ask me questions!

> ELINOR
> You have no confidence in me.

MARIANNE

This reproach from you! You, who confide in no one.

ELINOR

I have nothing to tell.

MARIANNE

Nor I. We have neither of us anything to tell. I because I conceal nothing and you because you communicate nothing.

109 INT. MRS JENNINGS'S HOUSE. BREAKFAST ROOM. DAY.

A silent breakfast. MARIANNE is red-eyed from crying and limp from lack of sleep. MRS JENNINGS is dressed to go out, pulling on her gloves and bustling as usual. PIGEON enters with a letter on a salver. He offers it to MARIANNE. She seizes it and runs out of the room. MRS JENNINGS chuckles.

MRS JENNINGS

There now! Lovers' quarrels are swift to heal! That letter will do the trick, mark my word.

She goes to the door.

MRS JENNINGS

I must be off. I hope he won't keep her waiting much longer, Miss Dashwood. It hurts to see her looking so forlorn.

She leaves and ELINOR finds herself alone with LUCY, who loses no time in sharing her new-found happiness.

LUCY

What a welcome I had from Edward's family, Miss Dashwood – I am surprised you never told me what an agreeable woman your sister-in-law is! And Mr Robert – all so affable!

ELINOR

It is perhaps fortunate that none of them knows of your engagement. Excuse me.

ELINOR rises and leaves.

---

110 INT. MRS JENNINGS'S HOUSE. BEDROOM. DAY.

ELINOR *finds* MARIANNE *sitting on the edge of the bed. She does not acknowledge* ELINOR *but merely lifts the letter and reads out, with deadly calm:*

MARIANNE

'My dear Madam – I am quite at a loss to discover in what point I could be so unfortunate as to offend you. My esteem for your family is very sincere but if I have given rise to a belief of more than I felt or meant to express, I shall reproach myself for not having been more guarded. My affections have long been engaged elsewhere and it is with great regret that I return your letters and the lock of hair which you so obligingly bestowed upon me. I am etc. John Willoughby.'

ELINOR

Oh, Marianne.

MARIANNE *gives a great howl of pain and flings herself across the bed as though in physical agony.*

ELINOR

Marianne, oh, Marianne – it is better to know at once what his intentions are. Dearest, think of what you would have felt if your engagement had carried on for months and months before he chose to put an end to it.

MARIANNE

We are not engaged.

ELINOR

But you wrote to him! I thought then that he must have left you with some kind of understanding?

MARIANNE

No – he is not so unworthy as you think him.

ELINOR

Not so unworthy! Did he tell you that he loved you?

MARIANNE

Yes. No – never absolutely. It was every day implied, but never declared. Sometimes I thought it had been, but it never was. He has broken no vow.

ELINOR

He has broken faith with all of us, he made us all believe he loved you.

MARIANNE

He did! He did – he loved me as I loved him.

MRS JENNINGS *bursts through the door in her hat and coat, panting.*

MRS JENNINGS

I had to come straight up – how are you, Miss Marianne?

MARIANNE *begins to sob uncontrollably.*

MRS JENNINGS

Poor thing! She looks very bad. No wonder, Miss Dashwood, for it is but too true. I was told here in the street by Miss Morton, who is a great friend: he is to be married at the end of the month – to a Miss Grey with fifty thousand pounds. Well, said I, if 'tis true, then he is a good-for-nothing who has used my young friend abominably ill, and I wish with all my soul that his wife may plague his heart out!

She goes round the bed to comfort MARIANNE.

MRS JENNINGS

But he is not the only young man worth having, my dear, and with your pretty face you will never want for admirers.

MARIANNE *sobs even harder.*

———

MRS JENNINGS

Ah, me! She had better have her cry out and have done with it. I will go and look out something to tempt her – does she care for olives?

ELINOR

I cannot tell you.

MRS JENNINGS *leaves.* MARIANNE *seizes the letter again.*

MARIANNE

I cannot believe his nature capable of such cruelty!

ELINOR

Marianne, there is no excuse for him – this is his hand –

MARIANNE

But it cannot be his heart! Oh, Mamma! I want Mamma! Elinor, please take me home! Cannot we go tomorrow?

ELINOR

There is no one to take us.

MARIANNE

Cannot we hire a carriage?

ELINOR

We have no money – and indeed we owe Mrs Jennings more courtesy.

MARIANNE

All *she* wants is gossip and she only likes me because I supply it! Oh, God! I cannot endure to stay.

ELINOR

I will find a way. I promise.

111 INT. COFFEE-HOUSE. COVENT GARDEN. DAY.
FANNY, JOHN *and* ROBERT *are drinking chocolate together.*

ROBERT

Apparently they never were engaged.

FANNY

Miss Grey has fifty thousand pounds. Marianne is virtually
penniless.

JOHN

She cannot have expected him to go through with it. But I feel for
Marianne – she will lose her bloom and end a spinster like Elinor.
I think, my dear, we might consider having them to stay with us
for a few days – we are, after all, family, and my father . . .

He trails off. FANNY *exchanges an alarmed glance with* ROBERT. *She
thinks fast.*

FANNY

My love, I would ask them with all my heart, but I have already
asked Miss Steele for a visit and we cannot deprive Mrs
Jennings of all her company at once. We can invite your sisters
some other year, you know, and Miss Steele will profit far more
from your generosity – poor girl!

JOHN

That is very thoughtful, Fanny. We shall ask Elinor and
Marianne next year, then . . .

FANNY

Certainly!

112 EXT. JOHN AND FANNY'S TOWN HOUSE. LONDON STREET.
DAY.
MRS JENNINGS's *carriage stands outside. A liveried* FOOTMAN *opens the
door and* LUCY *steps out brandishing a new muff.*

115B INT. MRS JENNINGS'S HOUSE. BEDROOM. DAY.
MARIANNE *sits alone on the bed. Around her lie her notes to Willoughby,
her lock of hair and the pocket sonnets. In her hands is the creased and tear-
stained letter from Willoughby which she is examining over and over.*

———

114 INT. MRS JENNINGS'S HOUSE. DRAWING ROOM. DAY.

ELINOR *is seated at a desk writing a letter. There is a sudden rap at the front door. Footsteps are heard and as she turns, the maid enters with* COLONEL BRANDON. ELINOR *rises to greet him.*

> ELINOR
> Thank you for coming, Colonel.

He bows. ELINOR *is on edge.* BRANDON *looks haggard with concern.*

> COLONEL BRANDON
> How does your sister?

> ELINOR
> I must get her home as quickly as possible. The Palmers can take us as far as Cleveland, which is but a day from Barton –

> COLONEL BRANDON
> Then permit me to accompany you and take you straight on from Cleveland to Barton myself.

ELINOR *takes his hands gratefully.*

> ELINOR
> I confess that is precisely what I had hoped for. Marianne suffers cruelly, and what pains me most is how hard she tries to justify Mr Willoughby. But you know her disposition.

After a moment BRANDON *nods. He seems unable to remain still or calm and finds it difficult to begin speaking.*

> COLONEL BRANDON
> Perhaps I – my regard for you all – Miss Dashwood, will you allow me to prove it by relating some circumstances which nothing but an earnest desire of being useful –

> ELINOR
> You have something to tell me of Mr Willoughby.

COLONEL BRANDON (*nods*)

When I quitted Barton last – but I must go further back. A short account of myself will be necessary. No doubt . . . no doubt Mrs Jennings has apprised you of certain events in my past – the sad outcome of my connection with a young woman named Eliza.

ELINOR *nods*.

COLONEL BRANDON

What is *not* commonly known is that twenty years ago, Eliza bore an illegitimate child. The father, whoever he was, abandoned them.

This is strong stuff. ELINOR's *concern deepens.*

COLONEL BRANDON

As she lay dying, she begged me to look after the child. Eliza died in my arms, broken, wasted away – ah! Miss Dashwood, such a subject – untouched for so many years – it is dangerous . . .

He paces about, barely able to conceal his distress.

COLONEL BRANDON

I had failed Eliza in every other way – I could not refuse her now. I took the child – Beth is her name – and placed her with a family where I could be sure she would be well looked after. I saw her whenever I could. I saw that she was headstrong like her mother – and, God forgive me, I indulged her, I allowed her too much freedom. Almost a year ago, she disappeared.

ELINOR

Disappeared!

COLONEL BRANDON

I instigated a search but for eight months I was left to imagine the worst. At last, on the day of the Delaford picnic, I received

---

111

the first news of her. She was with child . . . and the blackguard who had –

BRANDON *stops and looks straight at* ELINOR.

ELINOR
Good God. Do you mean – Willoughby?

BRANDON *nods.* ELINOR *drops into a chair, utterly shocked.*

COLONEL BRANDON
Before I could return to confront him, Lady Allen learned of his behaviour and turned him from the house. He beat a hasty retreat to London –

ELINOR
Yes! He left us that morning, without any explanation!

COLONEL BRANDON
Lady Allen had annulled his legacy. He was left with next to nothing, and in danger of losing all that remained to his debtors –

ELINOR
– and so abandoned Marianne for Miss Grey and her fifty thousand pounds.

BRANDON *is silent.* ELINOR *is breathless.*

ELINOR
Have you seen Mr Willoughby since you learned . . .?

BRANDON (*nodding*)
We met by appointment, he to defend, I to punish his conduct.

ELINOR *stares at him, aghast.*

BRANDON
We returned unwounded, so the meeting never got abroad.

ELINOR *nods and is silent for a moment.*

———

ELINOR

Is Beth still in town?

COLONEL BRANDON

She has chosen to go into the country for her confinement. Such has been the unhappy resemblance between the fate of mother and daughter, and so imperfectly have I discharged my trust.

A pause.

COLONEL BRANDON

I would not have burdened you, Miss Dashwood, had I not from my heart believed it might, in time, lessen your sister's regrets.

BRANDON *moves to the door and then stops. He turns to her and speaks with effort.*

COLONEL BRANDON

I have described Mr Willoughby as the worst of libertines – but I have since learned from Lady Allen that he did mean to propose that day. Therefore I cannot deny that his intentions towards Marianne *were* honourable, and I feel certain he would have married her, had it not been for –

ELINOR

For the money.

She looks up at BRANDON. *Silence.*

115 INT. MRS JENNINGS'S HOUSE. BEDROOM. NIGHT.
MARIANNE *is sitting on the bed staring into space.* ELINOR *is kneeling by her, holding her hands.*

ELINOR

Dearest, was I right to tell you?

113

MARIANNE

Of course.

ELINOR

Whatever his past actions, whatever his present course, at least you may be certain that he loved you.

MARIANNE

But not enough. Not enough.

115A INT. MRS JENNINGS'S HOUSE. STUDY. DAY.
ELINOR *sits alone with her head in her hands. Suddenly* MRS JENNINGS *bustles in looking pleased.*

MRS JENNINGS

Here is someone to cheer you up, Miss Dashwood!

She is followed in by LUCY. MRS JENNINGS *leaves, busy as ever.* LUCY *plants an expression of ghastly concern on her face.*

LUCY

How is your dear sister, Miss Dashwood? Poor thing! I must say, I do not know what I should do if a man treated me with so little respect.

ELINOR

I hope you are enjoying your stay with John and Fanny, Miss Steele?

LUCY

I was never so happy in my entire life, Miss Dashwood! I do believe your sister-in-law has taken quite a fancy to me. I had to come and tell you – for you cannot *imagine* what has happened!

ELINOR

No, I cannot.

LUCY

Yesterday I was introduced to Edward's mother!

———

114

ELINOR

Indeed?

LUCY

And she was a vast deal more than civil. I have not yet seen
Edward but now I feel sure to very soon –

The MAID *comes back.*

MAID

There's a Mr Edward Ferrars to see you, Miss Dashwood.

There is a tiny frozen silence.

ELINOR

Do ask him to come up.

ELINOR *quite involuntarily sits down and then stands up again.* EDWARD
is admitted, looking both anxious and eager. As LUCY *is sitting in the
window seat, at first he sees only* ELINOR.

EDWARD

Miss Dashwood, how can I –

But ELINOR *cuts him off.*

ELINOR

Mr Ferrars, what a pleasure to see you. You . . . know Miss
Steele, of course.

EDWARD *turns slowly and encounters* LUCY's *glassy smile. He all but
blenches. Then bows, and clears his throat.*

EDWARD

How do you do, Miss Steele.

LUCY

I am well, thank you, Mr Ferrars.

EDWARD *has no notion of what to do or say. He swallows.*

———

115

ELINOR

Do sit down, Mr Ferrars.

LUCY's *eyes are sharp as broken glass.* EDWARD *remains on his feet, looking helplessly from one woman to the other.*

LUCY

You must be surprised to find me here, Mr Ferrars! I expect you thought I was at your sister's house.

This is precisely what EDWARD *had thought. He tries to smile but his facial muscles won't work.* ELINOR *decides to fetch help.*

ELINOR

Let me call Marianne, Mr Ferrars. She would be most disappointed to miss you.

ELINOR *goes to the door, thankful to escape, but* MARIANNE *prevents her by walking in at that moment. Despite her anguish, she is very pleased to see* EDWARD *and embraces him warmly.*

MARIANNE

Edward! I heard your voice! At last you have found us!

EDWARD *is shocked by her appearance and momentarily forgets his own confusion.*

EDWARD

Forgive me, Marianne, my visit is shamefully overdue. You are pale. I hope you have not been unwell?

MARIANNE

Oh, don't think of me – Elinor is well, you see, that must be enough for both of us!

MARIANNE *gestures to* ELINOR *encouragingly but* EDWARD *seems unable to look at her.*

———

116

EDWARD

How do you like London, Marianne?

MARIANNE

Not at all. The sight of you is all the pleasure it has afforded, is that not so, Elinor?

Again, MARIANNE *endeavours to ignite the lovers.* ELINOR *tries to silence* MARIANNE *with her eyes but to no avail.* MARIANNE *puts their coolness down to the presence of* LUCY, *at whom she glances with a none too friendly air.*

MARIANNE

Why have you taken so long to come and see us?

EDWARD

I have been much engaged elsewhere.

MARIANNE

Engaged elsewhere! But what was that when there were such friends to be met?

LUCY

Perhaps, Miss Marianne, you think young men never honour their engagements, little or great.

ELINOR *is appalled by this remark but* MARIANNE *does not notice it and turns back to* LUCY *earnestly.*

MARIANNE

No, indeed – for Edward is the most fearful of giving pain and the most incapable of being selfish of anyone I ever saw.

EDWARD *makes an uncomfortable noise.*

MARIANNE

Edward, will you not sit? Elinor, help me to persuade him.

Now EDWARD *can stand it no longer.*

———

EDWARD

Forgive me but I must take my leave –

MARIANNE

But you are only just arrived!

ELINOR *rises, desperate for them both to go.*

EDWARD

You must excuse me, I have a commission to attend to for Fanny –

LUCY *jumps in like a shot.*

LUCY

In that case perhaps you might escort me back to your sister's house, Mr Ferrars?

There is an extremely awkward pause.

EDWARD

I would be honoured. Goodbye, Miss Dashwood, Miss Marianne.

He shakes hands with ELINOR *and with* MARIANNE, *who is silent with dismay.* LUCY *takes* EDWARD's *arm and looks up at him proprietorially. After a stiff bow and a muttered farewell from* EDWARD, *they leave.* MARIANNE *looks at her sister in astonishment.*

MARIANNE

Why did you not urge him to stay?

ELINOR

He must have had his reasons for going.

MARIANNE

His reason was no doubt your coldness. If I were Edward I would assume you did not care for me at all.

---

117 EXT. JOHN AND FANNY'S TOWN HOUSE. BACK GARDEN.
DAY.
A tranquil afternoon . . .

118 INT. JOHN AND FANNY'S TOWN HOUSE. DRAWING ROOM.
DAY.
LUCY *is sitting with* FANNY, *who is doing some pointless basketwork.*
LUCY *hands* FANNY *rushes.*

LUCY

Poor Miss Marianne looked very badly t'other day. When I
think of her, deserted and abandoned, it frightens me to think I
shall never marry.

FANNY

Nonsense. You will marry far better than either of the Dashwood girls.

LUCY

How can that possibly be?

FANNY

You have ten times their sense and looks.

LUCY

But I have no dowry.

FANNY

There are qualities which will always make up for that, and you
have them in abundance. It would not surprise me if you were
to marry far and away beyond your expectations.

LUCY

I wish it might be so. There is a young man –

FANNY

Ah ha! I am glad to hear of it. Is he of good breeding and
fortune?

LUCY

Oh both – but his family would certainly oppose the match.

FANNY

Tush! They will allow it as soon as they see you, my dear.

LUCY

It is a very great secret. I have told no one in the world for fear of discovery.

FANNY *looks up, curious to know more.*

FANNY

My dear, I am the soul of discretion.

LUCY

If I dared tell . . .

FANNY

I can assure you I am as silent as the grave.

LUCY *leans forward to whisper in* FANNY's *ear.*

119 EXT. JOHN AND FANNY'S TOWN HOUSE. DAY.
We hold a long shot of the house for a moment of silence. Then from inside comes an almost inhumanly loud shriek.

FANNY (V/O)

Viper in my bosom!

120 EXT. JOHN AND FANNY'S TOWN HOUSE. BACK GARDEN. DAY.
FANNY *is trying to drag* LUCY *out of the house.* ROBERT *and* JOHN *are trying to reason with her.* FANNY *loses her grip and falls backwards.* LUCY *flings herself into* ROBERT's *arms.* ROBERT *falls over.*

121 EXT. LONDON STREET. DAY.
MRS JENNINGS *is running as fast as her fat little legs will carry her.*

———

122 EXT. MRS JENNINGS'S HOUSE. BERKELEY STREET. DAY.
MRS JENNINGS *pants up the front steps.*

123 INT. MRS JENNINGS'S HOUSE. BEDROOM. DAY.
ELINOR *and* MARIANNE *are packing. Their mood is gloomy and uncommunicative.* MRS JENNINGS *explodes into the room fighting for breath.*

> **MRS JENNINGS**
> Oh, my dears! What a commotion! Mr Edward Ferrars – the very one I used to joke *you* about, Miss Dashwood – has been engaged these five years to Lucy Steele!

MARIANNE *lets out a gasp. She looks at* ELINOR, *who nods at her in swift confirmation.*

> **MRS JENNINGS**
> Poor Mr Ferrars! His mother, who by all accounts is very proud, demanded that he break the engagement on pain of disinheritance. But he has refused to break his promise to Lucy. He has stood by her, good man, and is cut off without a penny! She has settled it all irrevocably upon Mr Robert. But I cannot stop, I must go to Lucy. Your sister-in-law scolded her like any fury – drove her to hysterics . . .

She leaves the room, still rabbiting on. There is a silence.

> **MARIANNE**
> How long have you known?

> **ELINOR**
> Since the evening Mrs Jennings offered to take us to London.

> **MARIANNE**
> Why did you not tell me?

> **ELINOR**
> Lucy told me in the strictest confidence.

MARIANNE *looks at her in complete incredulity.*

> ELINOR
>
> I could *not* break my word.

Clearly, there is no arguing this point.

> MARIANNE
>
> But Edward loves *you.*

> ELINOR
>
> He made me no promises. He tried to tell me about Lucy.

> MARIANNE
>
> He cannot marry her.

> ELINOR
>
> Would you have him treat her even worse than Willoughby has treated you?

> MARIANNE
>
> No – but nor would I have him marry where he does not love.

ELINOR *tries hard to be controlled.*

> ELINOR
>
> Edward made his promise a long time ago, long before he met me. Though he may . . . harbour some regret, I believe he will be happy – in the knowledge that he did his duty and kept his word. After all – after all that is bewitching in the idea of one's happiness depending entirely on one person, it is not always possible. We must accept. Edward will marry Lucy – and you and I will go home.

> MARIANNE
>
> Always resignation and acceptance! Always prudence and honour and duty! Elinor, where is your heart?

ELINOR *finally explodes. She turns upon* MARIANNE *almost savagely.*

———

ELINOR

What do you know of my heart? What do you know of anything but your own suffering? For weeks, Marianne, I have had this pressing on me without being at liberty to speak of it to a single creature. It was forced upon me by the very person whose prior claims ruined all my hopes. I have had to endure her exultation again and again while knowing myself to be divided from Edward forever. Believe me, Marianne, had I not been bound to silence I could have produced proof enough of a broken heart even for you.

Complete silence. Then MARIANNE *speaks in a whisper.*

MARIANNE

Oh, Elinor!

MARIANNE *bursts into sobs and flings her arms around* ELINOR, *who, almost impatiently, tries to comfort her.*

124 EXT. PALMER RESIDENCE. LONDON STREET. DAY.

LUCY *and* MRS JENNINGS *are on the doorstep.* LUCY *looks rather lost and pathetic, with her little bundles, hastily packed. The door opens and* CHARLOTTE *precedes the* SERVANT, *ushering them in with shrill cries of sympathy.*

COLONEL BRANDON (V/O)

I have heard that your friend Mr Ferrars has been entirely cast off by his family for persevering in his engagement to Miss Steele . . .

125 EXT. SQUARE IN FRONT OF MRS JENNINGS'S HOUSE. LONDON. DAY.

ELINOR *and* BRANDON *walk round the quiet square.*

COLONEL BRANDON (*cont.*)

Have I been rightly informed? Is it so?

ELINOR *is greatly taken aback by this unexpected query.*

ELINOR

It is indeed so. Are you acquainted with Mr Ferrars?

COLONEL BRANDON

No, we have never met. But I know only too well the cruelty –
the *impolitic* cruelty of dividing two young people long attached
to one another. Mrs Ferrars does not know what she may drive
her son to –

He pauses, frowning in remembrance. ELINOR *waits in suspense.*

COLONEL BRANDON

I have a proposal to make that should enable him to marry Miss
Steele immediately. Since the gentleman is so close a friend to
your family, perhaps you will be good enough to mention it to
him?

ELINOR *is completely taken aback. She takes a moment to reply.*

ELINOR

Colonel, I am sure he would be only too delighted to hear it
from your own lips.

COLONEL BRANDON

I think not. His behaviour has proved him proud – in the best
sense. I feel certain this is the right course.

126 INT. MRS JENNINGS'S HOUSE. STUDY. DAY.

ELINOR *is waiting. The* MAID *announces* EDWARD *and he walks in
momentarily. They are alone for the first time in months and for a moment,
neither speaks.*

ELINOR

Mr Ferrars.

EDWARD

Miss Dashwood.

———

ELINOR *indicates a seat for him but neither sits.*

ELINOR
Thank you for responding so promptly to my message.

EDWARD
I was most grateful to receive it. I – Miss Dashwood, God knows what you must think of me . . .

ELINOR
Mr Ferrars –

He interrupts her, desperate to explain.

EDWARD
I have no right to speak, I know –

ELINOR *has to stop him.*

ELINOR
Mr Ferrars, I have good news. I think you know of our friend Colonel Brandon?

EDWARD *looks completely bewildered.*

EDWARD
Yes, I have heard his name.

ELINOR *starts to speak rather faster than usual.*

ELINOR
Colonel Brandon desires me to say that, understanding you wish to join the clergy, he has great pleasure in offering you the parish on his estate at Delaford, now just vacant, in the hope that it may enable you – and Miss Steele – to marry.

EDWARD *cannot at first take it in.* ELINOR *sits down.*

EDWARD
Colonel Brandon?

———

ELINOR

Yes. He means it as testimony of his concern for – for the cruel situation in which you find yourselves.

Now EDWARD *sits – in shock.*

EDWARD

Colonel Brandon give *me* a parish? Can it be possible?

ELINOR

The unkindness of your family has made you astonished to find friendship elsewhere.

EDWARD *looks at* ELINOR, *his eyes full of growing comprehension.*

EDWARD

No. Not to find it in you. I cannot be ignorant that to you – to your goodness – I owe it all. I feel it. I would express it if I could, but, as you know, I am no orator.

ELINOR

You are very much mistaken. I assure you that you owe it almost entirely to your own merit – I have had no hand in it.

But EDWARD *clearly believes she has been instrumental in the offer. He frowns slightly before speaking with rather an effort.*

EDWARD

Colonel Brandon must be a man of great worth and respect-ability.

ELINOR *finds some relief in saying at least one thing that she truly means.*

ELINOR

He is the kindest and best of men.

This makes EDWARD *seem even more depressed. He sits silent for a moment but then rouses himself to action.*

———

EDWARD

May I enquire why the Colonel did not tell me himself?

ELINOR

I think he felt it would be better coming from . . . a friend.

EDWARD *looks at* ELINOR, *his eyes full of sadness.*

EDWARD

Your friendship has been the most important of my life.

ELINOR

You will always have it.

EDWARD

Forgive me.

ELINOR

Mr Ferrars, you honour your promises – that is more important than anything else. I wish you – both – very happy.

They rise. She curtsies. He bows.

EDWARD

Goodbye, Miss Dashwood.

EDWARD *leaves silently.* ELINOR *stands stock-still in the middle of the room.*

127 EXT. MRS JENNINGS'S HOUSE. DAY.
The PALMERS' *carriage stands outside the house.* COLONEL BRANDON *helps* MARIANNE *in beside* ELINOR *before mounting his horse to ride alongside.* MRS JENNINGS *waves goodbye from the steps. The carriage moves off.* MRS JENNINGS *blows her nose, looks up and down the street in search of gossip and goes back indoors with a sigh.*

128 INT. THE PALMERS' CARRIAGE. ON THE ROAD. DAY.
MARIANNE *is sitting back in her seat with her eyes closed. She does not look well.* MR PALMER *is behind his newspaper.*

CHARLOTTE

What a stroke of luck for Lucy and Edward to find a parish so close to Barton! You will all be able to meet very often. That will cheer you up, Miss Marianne. I do declare I have never disliked a person so much as I do Mr Willoughby, for your sake. Insufferable man! To think we can see his insufferable house from the top of our hill!

CLOSE *on* MARIANNE's *eyes slowly opening.*

CHARLOTTE

I shall ask Jackson to plant some very tall trees.

MR PALMER (*from behind the paper*)
You will do nothing of the sort.

129 EXT. THE PALMERS' CARRIAGE. OPEN ROAD. DAY.
The carriage bowls along, with BRANDON *riding next to it.*

CHARLOTTE (V/O)
I hear Miss Grey's bridal gown was everything of the finest – made in Paris, no less. I should have liked to see it, although I dare say it was a sorry affair, scalloped with ruffles – but what do the French know about fashion?

130 EXT. CLEVELAND. DRIVE. AFTERNOON.
The carriage stands outside the PALMER *residence, a resplendent affair with a great deal of land.* BRANDON *is helping* MARIANNE *and* ELINOR *out of the carriage.*

CHARLOTTE (V/O)
I am resolved never to mention Mr Willoughby's name again, and furthermore I shall tell everyone I meet what a good-for-nothing he is.

MR PALMER (V/O)
Be quiet.

ELINOR *and* MARIANNE *stand on the steps as the* PALMERS *debouch from the carriage amid a welter of* SERVANTS.

ELINOR *(sotto voce)*
I do not think she drew breath from the moment we left London. It is my fault – I should have found some other way of getting home.

MARIANNE
There was no other way – you said so yourself.

ELINOR
We shall be home soon enough. Mamma will comfort you, dearest.

MARIANNE
I am stiff from sitting so long. Will you tell Charlotte that I am going for a stroll?

ELINOR *glances at the sky in concern.*

ELINOR
I think it is going to rain.

MARIANNE
No, no, it will not rain.

ELINOR *cannot help but smile at this return of the old* MARIANNE.

ELINOR
You always say that and then it always does.

MARIANNE
I will keep to the garden, near the house.

MARIANNE *walks off.* ELINOR *watches her go anxiously.*

132 INT. CLEVELAND. DRAWING ROOM. DAY.
MRS BUNTING, *a rather baleful* NANNY, *looks on as* MR PALMER *holds up a screaming* BABY *in a frilly bonnet for everyone's inspection.*

———

CHARLOTTE

We are very proud of our little Thomas, Colonel – and his papa
has such a way with him . . .

BRANDON *flicks a glance at* MR PALMER *for whom holding a baby comes
as naturally as breathing underwater.*

133 EXT. CLEVELAND. GARDEN. DAY.
MARIANNE *walks purposefully towards the garden wall, beyond which lies
a hill.*

134 INT. CLEVELAND. DRAWING ROOM. DAY.
ELINOR *enters to find* CHARLOTTE *alone with the now hysterical* BABY
THOMAS.

CHARLOTTE

There you are, Miss Dashwood! Mr Palmer and the Colonel
have locked themselves up in the billiard room. Come and meet
little Thomas. Where is Miss Marianne?

ELINOR

She is taking a little air in the garden.

CHARLOTTE

Oh, very good. That is the great advantage of the countryside –
all the fresh air and . . . and all the fresh air . . .

CHARLOTTE'S *conversational difficulties are drowned out by her offspring.*

135 EXT. CLEVELAND. GARDEN. DAY.
MARIANNE *comes to a gate in the wall and turns the handle. It opens. She
throws a glance back to the house and passes through. There is a low rumble
of thunder.*

136 INT. CLEVELAND. DRAWING ROOM. DAY.
BABY THOMAS *is purple in the face but shows no signs of quietening.*
CHARLOTTE *joggles him about inefficiently.*

———

130

CHARLOTTE (*yelling*)

He is the best child in the world – he never cries unless he wants to and then, Lord, there is no stopping him.

137 EXT. THE HILL. DAY.

MARIANNE, *calm and determined, walks towards the top of the hill. The wind whips and plucks at her hair and skirts.*

138 INT. CLEVELAND. DRAWING ROOM. DAY.

ELINOR, *traumatised by her new acquaintance with the shrieking BABY THOMAS, goes to look out of the window. She frowns.*

139 EXT. CLEVELAND. GARDEN. DAY.

ELINOR's POV. MARIANNE *is nowhere in sight. Storm clouds have gathered on the hill.*

140 INT. CLEVELAND. DRAWING ROOM. DAY.

ELINOR *turns from the window.* BABY THOMAS *stops crying for two seconds.*

ELINOR

I cannot see Marianne.

There is a crack of thunder. BABY THOMAS *starts again.*

141 EXT. THE HILL. DAY.

Rain has started to pour down. MARIANNE *walks on regardless.*

142 INT. CLEVELAND. DRAWING ROOM. DAY.

CHARLOTTE *shouts over* BABY THOMAS *to* ELINOR.

CHARLOTTE

She has probably taken shelter in one of the greenhouses!

143 EXT. THE HILL. DAY.

MARIANNE *has reached the top. Soaked to the skin, she stands with the storm raging around her, staring at the spires of Combe Magna, the place that would have been her home. Rain streaks her face and the wind whips her hair about her. Through frozen lips she whispers:*

———

MARIANNE

Love is not love
Which alters when it alteration finds
Or bends with the remover to remove:
O, no! it is an ever-fixed mark
That looks on tempests and is never shaken . . .

144 EXT. CLEVELAND. GREENHOUSES. DAY.
BRANDON *is looking for* MARIANNE. *He enters a greenhouse.*

COLONEL BRANDON
Marianne!

145 EXT. THE HILL. DAY.
MARIANNE *stares at Combe Magna, a strange smile playing about her lips. Then she calls to* WILLOUGHBY *as though he were near. The effect is eerie, unworldly.*

MARIANNE
Willoughby . . . Willoughby . . .

146 INT. CLEVELAND. DRAWING ROOM. DAY.
CHARLOTTE, MR PALMER *and* ELINOR *are waiting anxiously.* BABY THOMAS *has been removed.* ELINOR *is staring out of the window.*

CHARLOTTE
One thing is certain – she will be wet through when she returns.

MR PALMER
Thank you for pointing that out, my dear. Do not worry, Miss Dashwood – Brandon will find her. I think we can all guess where she went.

147 EXT. THE HILL. DAY.
BRANDON *runs up the hillside as though the devil were at his heels.*

148 INT. CLEVELAND. DRAWING ROOM. DAY.
CHARLOTTE *is handing* ELINOR *a cup of tea.* ELINOR *turns back to look out of the window. She freezes.*

149 EXT. CLEVELAND. GARDEN. DAY.
ELINOR's POV *of* BRANDON *walking up to the house with* MARIANNE *cradled in his arms. It is like seeing Willoughby's ghost.*

150 INT. CLEVELAND. HALL. DAY.
Everyone rushes out of the drawing room as the COLONEL *enters with* MARIANNE. *He is exhausted and soaked.* MARIANNE *is dumb with cold and fatigue.*

COLONEL BRANDON
She is not hurt – but we must get her warm!

ELINOR *and* MR PALMER *take* MARIANNE *from* BRANDON *and go upstairs, with* CHARLOTTE *in pursuit.*

151 EXT. CLEVELAND. NIGHT. RAIN.
The great house sits in darkness. A sense of foreboding.

152 INT. CLEVELAND. UPSTAIRS CORRIDOR. NIGHT.
ELINOR *is in her nightgown, knocking at a door.* MR PALMER *answers in his nightshirt, astonished to have been summoned out of bed.*

ELINOR
I think Marianne may need a doctor.

153 INT. CLEVELAND. BREAKFAST ROOM. DAY.
MR PALMER *and* CHARLOTTE *are sitting at the breakfast table.* BRANDON *is pacing. The rain has stopped.*

CHARLOTTE
You'll wear yourself out, Colonel! Do not worry! A day or two in bed will soon set her to rights!

———

MR PALMER

You can rely upon Harris, Colonel. I have never found a better physician.

Enter ELINOR *with* DR HARRIS.

COLONEL BRANDON (*urgent*)

What is your diagnosis?

DR HARRIS

It is an infectious fever that has taken far more serious hold than I would have expected in one so young. I would recommend the hasty removal of your child, Mr Palmer –

CHARLOTTE *runs out of the room screaming.*

CHARLOTTE

Mrs Bunting! Mrs Bunting!

154 EXT. CLEVELAND. FRONT STEPS. DAY.
CHARLOTTE *is getting into their carriage with* MRS BUNTING *and* BABY THOMAS. MR PALMER *is on the steps with* ELINOR. *He takes her hand and looks at her with real sympathy.*

MR PALMER

My dear Miss Dashwood, I am more sorry than I can say. If you would prefer me to stay I am at your service.

ELINOR *is touched to find this warm heart beneath his frosty exterior.*

ELINOR

Mr Palmer, that is very kind. But Colonel Brandon and Dr Harris will look after us. Thank you for everything you have done.

MR PALMER *nods, presses her hand, and walks down the steps to the carriage.*

———

155 INT. CLEVELAND. DRAWING ROOM. DAY.
BRANDON *sits head in hands. His ghosts have come to haunt him.*

156. INT. CLEVELAND. ELINOR AND MARIANNE'S
BEDROOM. DAY.
MARIANNE *is tossing and turning in the bed.* DR HARRIS *is trying to take her pulse. He looks up at* ELINOR, *who is watching anxiously.*

> DR HARRIS
> She is not doing as well as I would like.

157 INT. CLEVELAND. UPSTAIRS CORRIDOR. DAY.
ELINOR *exits the bedroom to find* BRANDON *outside. She jumps.*

> COLONEL BRANDON
> What can I do?

> ELINOR
> Colonel, you have done so much already.

> COLONEL BRANDON
> Give me an occupation, Miss Dashwood, or I shall run mad.

He is dangerously quiet.

> ELINOR
> She would be easier if her mother were here.

> COLONEL BRANDON
> Of course. Barton is but eight hours away. If I make no stop, you may see us early tomorrow morning.

He takes ELINOR's *hand and kisses it.*

> COLONEL BRANDON
> In your hands I know she will be safe.

158 EXT. CLEVELAND. DRIVE. EVE.
BRANDON *mounts his horse, turns to look at the house for a moment, and then spurs it violently forward.*

---

159 INT. CLEVELAND. ELINOR AND MARIANNE'S BEDROOM. EVE.
ELINOR *is by the window, having watched* BRANDON's *departure. DR
HARRIS is by* MARIANNE's *side. He turns to* ELINOR.

DR HARRIS
Double the number of drops and I will return as soon as I can.

160 EXT. CLEVELAND. NIGHT.
*The house stands in virtual darkness with only a dim light issuing from one
of the upper rooms.*

161 EXT. OPEN ROAD. NIGHT.
BRANDON *riding fast, his cape billowing out behind him.*

162 INT. CLEVELAND. ELINOR AND MARIANNE'S BEDROOM.
NIGHT.
MARIANNE's *eyes glitter with the fever.* ELINOR *wipes her brow.
Suddenly she speaks.*

MARIANNE
Who is that?

She is looking at the end of the bed.

MARIANNE
Look, look, Elinor.

ELINOR
There is no one there, dearest.

MARIANNE
It is Papa. Papa has come.

ELINOR *looks fearfully towards the end of the bed.* MARIANNE *tries to
smile with her cracked lips.*

MARIANNE
Dearest Papa!

The dead are coming for the dying.

DISSOLVE.

163 INT. CLEVELAND. ELINOR AND MARIANNE'S BEDROOM.
LATER.
ELINOR, *her eyes red from watching, wipes* MARIANNE's *temples.* DR
HARRIS *takes her pulse and looks at* ELINOR *anxiously. His silence is
worse than any utterance.*

DISSOLVE.

164 INT. CLEVELAND. ELINOR AND MARIANNE'S BEDROOM.
LATER.
The room is very still. MARIANNE *is pale as wax.* DR HARRIS *puts on his
coat.* ELINOR *looks at him fearfully.*

DR HARRIS
I must fetch more laudanum. I cannot pretend, Miss Dashwood,
that your sister's condition is not very serious. You must
prepare yourself. I will return very shortly.

He leaves the room.

DISSOLVE.

165 INT. CLEVELAND. ELINOR AND MARIANNE'S BEDROOM.
LATER.
MARIANNE *lies in the grip of her fever.* ELINOR *sits watching her. Slowly
she rises and walks to the bed. When she speaks, her tone is very practical.*

ELINOR
Marianne, Marianne, please try –

*Suddenly, almost unconsciously, she starts to heave with dry sobs, wrenched
out of her, full of anguish and heartbreak and all the more painful for being
tearless.*

137

ELINOR

Marianne, please try – I cannot – I cannot do without you. Oh,
please, I have tried to bear everything else – I will try – but
please, dearest, beloved Marianne, do not leave me alone . . .

*She falls to her knees by the bed, gulping for breath, taking MARIANNE's
hand and kissing it again and again.*

DISSOLVE.

166 EXT. CLEVELAND. GARDENS. DAWN.
*A shimmer of light appears on the rim of the horizon. Somewhere a lark
breaks into clear untroubled song.*

167 INT. CLEVELAND. ELINOR AND MARIANNE'S BEDROOM.
MORNING.
*DR HARRIS sits slumped in a chair. MARIANNE lies motionless.
ELINOR rises with difficulty from the bedside and goes to the window.
She is white as paper. The lark sings. Then, from behind, comes the faintest
of whispers.*

MARIANNE (V/O)

Elinor?

*ELINOR turns with a cry. DR HARRIS springs from his seat and examines
MARIANNE. He then turns to ELINOR with a smile of relief and nods. At
that moment the sound of carriage wheels is heard on the gravel.*

ELINOR

My mother!

168 EXT. CLEVELAND. FRONT STEPS. MORNING.
*BRANDON helps MRS DASHWOOD, who is weak with exhaustion and
distress, out of the carriage.*

169 INT. CLEVELAND. STAIRCASE. MORNING.
ELINOR hurls herself down the stairs. She reaches the door just as

———

BRANDON *and* MRS DASHWOOD *enter and practically swoons into her mother's arms.*

ELINOR
Mamma! She is out of danger!

170 INT. CLEVELAND. ELINOR AND MARIANNE'S BEDROOM. MORNING.
CLOSE *on* MARIANNE's *face as* MRS DASHWOOD *kisses her.*

MRS DASHWOOD
There, there, my love, my Marianne.

MARIANNE *opens her eyes and smiles at her mother.* MRS DASHWOOD *takes her gently into her arms.* MARIANNE *suddenly looks anxious. She is too weak to move her head. She whispers with urgent effort.*

MARIANNE
Where is Elinor?

ELINOR
I am here, dearest, I am here.

MARIANNE *looks at her with deep relief. Behind the* DASHWOODS, BRANDON *stands at the door, unwilling to intrude on this intimacy. He wipes his eyes and turns away.* MARIANNE *sees and whispers to him.*

MARIANNE
Colonel Brandon.

BRANDON *turns back, his eyes full of tears.* MARIANNE *looks at him for a moment. Then, very quietly:*

MARIANNE
Thank you.

171 EXT. BARTON COTTAGE. GARDEN AND SURROUNDINGS. DAY.
The cottage nestles in the first buds of spring. A piece of rope hangs down

---

from the branches of a tree in the garden. It starts to wave about wildly and we see MARGARET emerging and climbing down. She has built herself a new tree-house.

> COLONEL BRANDON (V/O)
> What though the sea with waves continuall
> Doe eate the earth, it is no more at all . . .

172 INT. BARTON COTTAGE. PARLOUR. DAY.

MARIANNE is on the sofa by the window. She is pale, convalescent and calm. Different somehow. She listens intently as BRANDON reads her the poem.

> COLONEL BRANDON
> Nor is the earth the lesse, or loseth aught.
> For whatsoever from one place doth fall,
> Is with the tide unto another brought . . .

We move back to find MRS DASHWOOD and ELINOR at the other end of the room, sewing peacefully.

> MRS DASHWOOD
> He certainly is not so dashing as Willoughby but he has a far more pleasing countenance. There was always a something, if you remember, in Willoughby's eyes at times which I did not like.

ELINOR listens patiently as her mother rewrites history. We cut back to BRANDON as he finishes reading.

> COLONEL BRANDON
> 'For there is nothing lost, but may be found, if sought . . .'

He looks up at MARIANNE. A soul-breathing glance. She smiles as he closes the book.

> MARIANNE
> Shall we continue tomorrow?

COLONEL BRANDON
No – for I must away.

MARIANNE
Away? Where?

COLONEL BRANDON (*teasing*)
That I cannot tell you. It is a secret.

He rises to leave.

MARIANNE (*impulsive*)
But you will not stay away long?

CLOSE *on* BRANDON's *reaction.*

172A EXT. FIELDS NEAR BARTON COTTAGE. DAY.
ELINOR *and* MARIANNE *are out on a walk. They go very slowly,*
MARIANNE *leaning on* ELINOR's *arm. Their mood is loving, companion-
able.*

173 EXT. DOWNS NEAR BARTON COTTAGE. DAY.
ELINOR *and* MARIANNE *walk on. Suddenly,* MARIANNE *stops.*

MARIANNE
There.

She indicates a spot on the ground but ELINOR *can see nothing and is
momentarily alarmed.* MARIANNE *gazes at the ground and breathes in
deeply.*

MARIANNE
There I fell, and there I first saw Willoughby.

ELINOR
Poor Willoughby. He will always regret you.

MARIANNE
But does it follow that, had he chosen me, he would have been
content?

———

ELINOR *looks at* MARIANNE, *surprised.*

MARIANNE
He would have had a wife he loved but no money – and might soon have learned to rank the demands of his pocket-book far above the demands of his heart.

ELINOR *regards* MARIANNE *admiringly.* MARIANNE *smiles sadly.*

MARIANNE
If his present regrets are half as painful as mine, he will suffer enough.

ELINOR
Do you compare your conduct with his?

MARIANNE
No. I compare it with what it ought to have been. I compare it with yours.

ELINOR
Our situations were very different.

MARIANNE
My illness has made me consider the past. I saw in my own behaviour nothing but imprudence – and worse. I was insolent and unjust to everyone –

ELINOR *tries to stem the flow but* MARIANNE *continues.*

MARIANNE
– but you – you I wronged above all. Only I knew your heart and its sorrows but even then I was never a grain more compassionate. I brought my illness upon myself – I wanted to destroy myself. And had I succeeded, what misery should I have caused you?

ELINOR *embraces her. They stand with their arms round one another in*

---

silence for a moment. Then MARIANNE breaks away and speaks with great good humour and energy.

MARIANNE

I shall mend my ways! I shall no longer worry others nor torture myself. I am determined to enter on a course of serious study – Colonel Brandon has promised me the run of his library and I shall read at least six hours a day. By the end of the year I expect to have improved my learning a very great deal.

174 EXT. ROAD NEAR BARTON COTTAGE. DAY.

THOMAS *is sitting on the back of a local wagon, holding a basket of food. He jumps off near the cottage and waves a cheery farewell to the* DRIVER.

175 INT. BARTON COTTAGE. PARLOUR. DAY.

CLOSE *on the accounts book, covered in blots and crossed-out sums. Pull up to reveal* MARIANNE *labouring over it. Her sickness has left her slightly short-sighted and she uses a pince-nez that makes her look like an owl.* ELINOR *is sewing and* MRS DASHWOOD *is snoozing.* MARGARET *goes up and looks over* MARIANNE's *shoulder. She frowns at the spider's web of ink.*

MARGARET

You'll go blind if you're not careful.

BETSY *brings in coals for the fire.* MRS DASHWOOD *rouses herself.*

MRS DASHWOOD

Is Thomas back from Exeter, Betsy?

BETSY

Yes, ma'am – he brung back two lovely fillets for you.

MRS DASHWOOD *looks nervously at* ELINOR *like a child who has been caught out.*

MRS DASHWOOD

Beef is far less expensive in Exeter, and anyway they are for Marianne.

ELINOR *laughs and rolls her eyes to heaven.* BETSY *turns on her way out to remark:*

BETSY

Sixpence a piece, Miss Dashwood. Oh, and he says Mr Ferrars is married, but I suppose you know that, ma'am.

There is a stunned silence. Everyone looks at ELINOR.

MRS DASHWOOD

Fetch Thomas to us, Betsy.

BETSY *leaves. They all sit very still.* MARGARET *is about to talk to* ELINOR *about it but* MARIANNE *stops her.* THOMAS *enters.*

THOMAS

Beg pardon, Miss Dashwood, but they was the cheapest in the market –

MRS DASHWOOD

It was a very good price, Thomas, well done. Would you be so kind as to build up the fire a little?

THOMAS (*relieved*)

Yes, ma'am.

There is a pause.

MRS DASHWOOD

Who told you that Mr Ferrars was married, Thomas?

THOMAS *builds up the fire as he answers. He tells the story with pleasure.*

———

THOMAS

I seen him myself, ma'am, and his lady too, Miss Lucy Steele as was – they were stopping in a chaise at the New London Inn. I happened to look up as I passed the chaise and I see it was Miss Steele. So I took off my hat and she enquired after you, ma'am, and all the young ladies, especially Miss Dashwood, and bid me I should give you her and Mr Ferrars's best compliments and service and how they'd be sure to send you a piece of the cake.

MRS DASHWOOD

Was Mr Ferrars in the carriage with her?

THOMAS

Yes, ma'am – I just seen him leaning back in it, but he did not look up.

ELINOR *screws up her courage.*

ELINOR

Did –

But she cannot continue. MARIANNE *glances at her compassionately and takes over.*

MARIANNE

Did Mrs Ferrars seem well?

THOMAS

Yes, Miss Marianne – she said how she was vastly contented and, since she was always a very affable young lady, I made free to wish her joy.

MRS DASHWOOD

Thank you, Thomas.

He nods and leaves, confused by the silent atmosphere. ELINOR *sits for a moment, then gets up and walks out.*

———

176 EXT. BARTON COTTAGE. GARDEN. EVE.

ELINOR *is standing by the gate, looking out.* MRS DASHWOOD *comes down the path to join her. She links arms with* ELINOR *and they stand in silence for a beat.*

> ### MRS DASHWOOD
> Your father once told me not to allow you to neglect yourself. Now I find that it is I who have neglected you most.

> ### ELINOR
> No, Mamma.

> ### MRS DASHWOOD
> Yes, I have. We all have. Marianne is right.

> ### ELINOR
> I am very good at hiding.

> ### MRS DASHWOOD
> Then we must observe you more closely.

A pause.

> ### ELINOR
> Mamma?

> ### MRS DASHWOOD
> Yes, my darling?

> ### ELINOR
> There is a painful difference between the expectation of an unpleasant event and its final certainty.

MRS DASHWOOD *squeezes* ELINOR's *arm tightly.*

177 EXT. OPEN ROAD NEAR BARTON. DAY.
A horse and cart are jogging along. The cart contains a large object tied down and covered with canvas. The DRIVER *whistles tunelessly.*

---

178 INT. BARTON COTTAGE. KITCHEN. DAY.

MARGARET *is standing on the kitchen table while* ELINOR *and* MAR-IANNE *pin a piece of material around the bottom of her skirt to lengthen it. Suddenly there is a commotion upstairs.*

> MRS DASHWOOD (V/O)
> Marianne! Marianne! Come and see what is coming!

Everyone runs out of the kitchen.

179 EXT. BARTON COTTAGE. GARDEN. DAY.

THOMAS *and the* CARTER *are carrying a small piano up the path.*

180 INT. BARTON COTTAGE. PARLOUR. DAY.

They carry the piano into the parlour and to the DASHWOODS' *joyful astonishment it fits perfectly.* MRS DASHWOOD *reads out the letter that has accompanied it.*

> MRS DASHWOOD
> 'At last I have found a small enough instrument to fit the parlour. I expect to follow it in a day or two, by which time I expect you to have learned the enclosed. Your devoted friend, Christopher Brandon.'

MRS DASHWOOD *hands* MARIANNE *the letter and a broadsheet song.*

> MARGARET
> He must like you very much, Marianne.

> MARIANNE
> It is not just for me! It is for all of us.

All the same, she looks conscious of the truth.

181 EXT. BARTON COTTAGE. GARDEN. DAY.

MARGARET *is up her tree.* ELINOR *is pulling weeds.* MRS DASHWOOD *is sitting on a stool working on* MARGARET's *dress and listening to the strains of the new song which* MARIANNE *is singing in the cottage. All of a*

---

sudden, MRS DASHWOOD *rises, shielding her eyes with her hand. She walks down to the gate, looking out.*

MRS DASHWOOD
Here is Colonel Brandon! Marianne!

The piano stops. MARIANNE *comes out and they all gather at the gate to watch for the rider.*

182 EXT. OPEN COUNTRY. DAY.
Their POV of a HORSEMAN in the distance.

183 EXT. BARTON COTTAGE. GARDEN GATE. DAY.
ELINOR
I do not think it *is* the Colonel.

MRS DASHWOOD
It must be. He said he would arrive today. You must play him the new song, Marianne.

Suddenly there is a yell from MARGARET's *tree.*

MARGARET
Edward!

MARGARET *practically throws herself out of the tree onto the grass.*

MARGARET
It is Edward!

The women look at each other in complete consternation.

MRS DASHWOOD
Calm. We must be calm.

184 INT. BARTON COTTAGE. PARLOUR. DAY.
Tense silence reigns. Everyone tries to busy themselves. BETSY *enters.*

BETSY
Mr Ferrars for you, ma'am.

EDWARD *follows her in, looking white and agitated.*

MRS DASHWOOD (*rising*)
Edward! What a pleasure to see you.

EDWARD
Mrs Dashwood. Miss Marianne. Margaret. Miss Dashwood. I
hope I find you all well.

He bows formally to each of them, lingering on ELINOR, *who is looking
firmly at her lap. He looks anxious.*

MARIANNE
Thank you, Edward, we are all very well.

There is a pause while they all search for an appropriate remark. Finally
MARGARET *decides to have a go at polite conversation.*

MARGARET
We have been enjoying very fine weather.

MARIANNE *looks at her incredulously.*

MARGARET
Well, we have.

EDWARD
I am glad of it. The . . . the roads were very dry.

MRS DASHWOOD *decides to bite the bullet.*

MRS DASHWOOD (*giving him her hand*)
May I wish you great joy, Edward.

*He takes her hand somewhat confusedly and accepts her offer of a seat.
There is an awful silence.* MARIANNE *tries to help.*

———

MARIANNE

I hope you have left Mrs Ferrars well?

EDWARD

Tolerably, thank you.

There is another bone-crunching pause.

EDWARD

I –

But EDWARD *cannot seem to find any words.*

MRS DASHWOOD

Is Mrs Ferrars at the new parish?

EDWARD *looks extremely confused.*

EDWARD

No – my mother is in town.

He plucks up the courage to look at ELINOR *again and is evidently not much comforted by what he sees.*

MRS DASHWOOD

I meant to enquire after Mrs Edward Ferrars.

EDWARD *colours. He hesitates.*

EDWARD

Then you have not heard – the news – I think you mean my brother – you mean Mrs Robert Ferrars.

They all stare at him in shock.

MRS DASHWOOD

Mrs Robert Ferrars?

ELINOR *has frozen.* EDWARD *rises and goes to the window.*

———

EDWARD

Yes. I received a letter from Miss Steele – or Mrs Ferrars, I should say – communicating the . . . the transfer of her affections to my brother Robert. They were much thrown together in London, I believe, and . . . and in view of the change in my circumstances, I felt it only fair that Miss Steele be released from our engagement. At any rate, they were married last week and are now in Plymouth.

ELINOR *rises suddenly,* EDWARD *turns and they stand looking at one another.*

ELINOR

Then you – are not married.

EDWARD

No.

ELINOR *bursts into tears. The shock of this emotional explosion stuns everyone for a second and then* MARIANNE *makes an executive decision. Wordlessly, she takes* MARGARET's *hand and leads her and* MRS DASHWOOD *out of the room.*

185 EXT. BARTON COTTAGE. GARDEN. DAY.
The three DASHWOODS *come into the garden, still holding hands.*

186 INT. BARTON COTTAGE. PARLOUR. DAY.
ELINOR *cannot stop crying.* EDWARD *comes forward, very slowly.*

EDWARD

Elinor! I met Lucy when I was very young. Had I had an active profession, I should never have felt such an idle, foolish inclination. At Norland my behaviour was very wrong. But I convinced myself you felt only friendship for me and it was my heart alone that I was risking. I have come with no expectations. Only to profess, now that I am at liberty to do so, that my heart is and always will be yours.

———

151

ELINOR *looks at him, her face streaked with tears of released emotion, of pain and of happiness.*

187 EXT. BARTON COTTAGE. GARDEN.
MARIANNE *and* MRS DASHWOOD *are stamping about in the garden trying to keep warm.* MARGARET *has climbed into her tree-house. The branches rustle.*

MARGARET
He's sitting next to her!

MRS DASHWOOD/MARIANNE
Margaret, come down!/Is he?

MRS DASHWOOD (*scolding*)
Margaret! Will you stop –

MARIANNE
What's happening now?

MRS DASHWOOD
Marianne!

MARGARET (V/O)
He's kneeling down!

MRS DASHWOOD *can't help herself.*

MRS DASHWOOD
Oh! Is he? Oh!

She and MARIANNE *look at each other joyfully.*

188 EXT. DOWNS NEAR BARTON. DAY.
The figures of EDWARD *and* ELINOR *can be seen walking, in deep conversation.*

———

189 EXT. PATH NEAR BARTON COTTAGE. DUSK.

Later. The lovers walk slowly, their heads almost touching, their words low and intimate.

ELINOR
Your mother, I suppose, will hardly be less angry with Robert for marrying Lucy.

EDWARD
The more so since she settled the money upon him so irrevocably –

ELINOR
– no doubt because she had run out of sons to disinherit.

EDWARD
Her family fluctuates at an alarming rate. Then, in London, when you told me of the Colonel's offer, I became convinced that *you* wanted me to marry Lucy and that – well, that you and Colonel Brandon . . .

ELINOR
Me and Colonel Brandon!

EDWARD
I shall not forget attempting to thank him for making it possible for me to marry the woman I did not love while convinced he had designs upon the woman I did – do – love.

EDWARD *stops walking. He looks at* ELINOR *and realises he can stand it no longer.*

EDWARD
Would you – can you – excuse me –

He takes her face in his hands and kisses her.

---

190 EXT. PATH TO BARTON CHURCH. DAY.

A group of VILLAGE CHILDREN *run down the hillside towards the church waving ribbons and dressed in their Sunday best.*

191 EXT. BARTON VILLAGE CHURCH. DAY.

A large wedding party is gathered outside the church. The entire village is present – CHILDREN, FARMERS, LABOURERS, SHOPKEEPERS, *and all our* PRINCIPALS. *We see* MRS JENNINGS *in a gigantic mauve bonnet,* CHARLOTTE *and* MR PALMER, SIR JOHN, MRS DASHWOOD, MARGARET, THOMAS, JOHN *and* FANNY, *who is dressed in a fantastically inappropriate concoction, and some* MEN *in regimental uniform. The path to the church is strewn with wild flowers and everyone holds a bunch of their own. The church bells start to peal, and a great cheer goes up as the door opens and* BETSY *comes out holding the bridal cake aloft. The bride and groom appear:* MARIANNE, *in white lawn, and* COLONEL BRANDON *in full uniform. Behind them come* EDWARD *in his parson's garb and, on his arm,* ELINOR *as matron of honour.* CLOSE *on them as they watch the party moving away.* MARIANNE *and* BRANDON *make their way forwards, everyone throws their flowers over them, whooping and singing.*

An open carriage decked with bridal wreaths comes to meet them, and BRANDON *lifts* MARIANNE *in. His melancholy air is all but gone and he radiates joyful life and vigour.* MARIANNE *also looks extremely happy – but there is a gravity to her joy that makes her seem much older.*

According to the custom of the time, BRANDON *throws a large handful of sixpences into the crowd, and the* VILLAGE CHILDREN *jump and dive for them.*

The coins spin and bounce, catching the sun like jewels. One hits FANNY *in the eye. She reels and falls over backwards into a gorse bush.* CAM *pulls back as the wedding procession makes its glorious way from the church. We draw away into the surrounding countryside. Then we see, on the far edge of frame, very small, a MAN sitting on a white horse, watching. It is WILLOUGHBY. As we draw back further still, he slowly pulls the horse around and moves off in the opposite direction.*

FILM CREDITS

COLUMBIA PICTURES Presents:

A Mirage Production
A Film by Ang Lee

Emma Thompson   Alan Rickman   Kate Winslet   Hugh Grant

Sense and Sensibility

James Fleet   Elizabeth Spriggs   Imelda Staunton
Harriet Walter   Robert Hardy   Imogen Stubbs
Gemma Jones   Greg Wise   Hugh Laurie

Adapted from the novel by Jane Austen
Casting by Michelle Guish
Music by Patrick Doyle
Costumes by Jenny Beavan and John Bright
Edited by Tim Squyres
Production Designer Luciana Arrighi
Director of Photography Michael Coulter BSC
Co-Producers James Schamus and Laurie Borg
Executive Producer Sydney Pollack
Screenplay by Emma Thompson
Produced by Lindsay Doran
Directed by Ang Lee

CAST
(In order of appearance)

John Dashwood	James Fleet
Mr Dashwood	Tom Wilkinson
Fanny Dashwood	Harriet Walter
Marianne Dashwood	Kate Winslet
Elinor Dashwood	Emma Thompson
Mrs Dashwood	Gemma Jones
Edward Ferrars	Hugh Grant
Margaret Dashwood	Emile François
Mrs Jennings	Elizabeth Spriggs
Sir John Middleton	Robert Hardy
Thomas	Ian Brimble
Betsy	Isabelle Amyes
Colonel Brandon	Alan Rickman
John Willoughby	Greg Wise
Curate	Alexander John
Charlotte Palmer	Imelda Staunton
Lucy Steele	Imogen Stubbs
Mr Palmer	Hugh Laurie
Pigeon	Allan Mitchell
Maid to Mrs Jennings	Josephine Gradwell
Robert Ferrars	Richard Lumsden
Miss Grey	Lone Vidahl
Doctor Harris	Oliver Ford Davies
Mrs Bunting	Eleanor McCready

———

EMMA THOMPSON won an Academy Award for Best Actress in 1992 for her portrayal of Margaret Schlegel in *Howards End* and was nominated twice in 1993 for her leading role in *The Remains of the Day* and her supporting role in *In the Name of the Father*.

Sense and Sensibility is her first screenplay.

Before graduating from Cambridge University in 1982 with a degree in English Literature, Thompson acted for three years with the Footlights at the Edinburgh Fringe; with Cambridge's first all-female revue *Woman's Hour*, which she co-wrote, co-produced and co-directed; and in her first solo show, *Short Vehicle*.

In London, Thompson starred opposite Robert Lindsay in the hit revival of *Me and My Girl*, and opposite Kenneth Branagh in John Osborne's *Look Back in Anger*, directed by Dame Judi Dench. For the Renaissance Theatre Company World Tour, she was directed by Branagh as the Fool in *King Lear*, and as Helena in *A Midsummer Night's Dream*. A BBC broadcast of the early Cambridge Footlights led to many other comedy appearances for Thompson, which culminated in *The Emma Thompson Special*. More dramatic work began with roles in the BBC six-hour mini-series *Tutti Frutti* and the seven-hour BBC series *Fortunes of War*, for which she won the BAFTA Best Actress award.

Thompson's additional film credits include *Junior, Much Ado About Nothing, Henry V, Dead Again, Peter's Friends*, and *Impromptu*. Most recently, she played the title role in Christopher Hampton's *Carrington*, which won a Special Jury Prize at the 1995 Cannes Festival.